HOLE IN THE MOON

by

STEVEN PANK

HOLE IN THE MOON
by
Steven Pank

Published by ABFree Publishing 2024
http://www.buffry.org.uk/abefreepublishing.html
ISBN 9781838440183
Revised September 2025

Thanks to Alun Buffry and ABeFree Publishing for
formatting the paperback.

CHAPTER 1

At the Space Centre it was a bright sunny day. Final preparations had been made, and the public viewing area was filled with people anticipating the launch of the Halliday rocket to the moon. An announcement was made to the crowd and to the media.

'The commentator: "This will prove to be a momentous expedition to the Moon. Starting with this launch today, it is to explore the availability of rare earth and other minerals. It is backed by the Halliday Mining Corporation, who are hoping to find those rare minerals on the Moon with a view to supplying the computer industry, the battery industry and the electric car industry, with all these much-needed materials and other resources."

Wearing light blue spacesuits, the Astronauts walked out onto a platform, all smiles.

The commentator: "Here's the four-person crew coming out now. In the team are the mineral expert and team leader, John Arland, the pilot, Andrew Stevenson, the navigator and astronomer, Julia Brownlow and the orbiter pilot David Jones. He will be piloting the orbiter and the other three will be going down onto the surface in the LEM, using a modified Lunar Rover that is equipped to detect materials on or close to the surface."

The crew entered the lift that took them up the gantry and climbed into the capsule on the top of the giant rocket.

After entering the cabin, the four astronauts settled down in their seats and waited as the various checks were announced. Then, before long, they could hear the countdown starting. As it got towards lift-off, they wriggled and moved slightly making themselves comfortable.

The lift-off began, the noise from the rocket engines built up to a roar. The monster spaceship steadily lifted off from the gantry in a cloud of flame and smoke and then headed up into the sky. The crew members in their rocket were now on their way to the Moon.

As the ship got higher and away from earth's gravity the crew members loosened their belts and started the routine of checking of the readings and the condition of the equipment.

Andrew was in communication with mission control and later Julia and David prepared and served some food in plastic bags.

It took just two days to approach the moon, things went normally as they eventually reached the point of entering lunar orbit.

David was controlling the orbiter and at the right

moment he gave the command for them to separate out in the LEM (Lunar Excursion Module) and after just one orbit of the Moon they prepared for the descent.

As they started to descend onto the surface, pilot Andrew Stevenson took over control for the last few feet of in order to find a safe landing area and they touched down.

After the landing they took time for a short rest before they prepared to leave the ship.

Wearing space suits, they descended the ladder one at a time and looked around.

Andrew and Julia started unloading the Moon Rover from the Lunar module, while John scanned the ground using a piece of equipment like a metal detector around the area near the landing site

Julia chose the area for their first scan. She had worked out that they could cover an area 150 feet by 300 feet in 6 sweeps.

As they set off, John spoke into recording equipment about what the Rover was tracking on the surface or below the ground. This was estimated to have taken about 30 minutes.

They returned from that run and Julia suggested the next run should be beyond that and went a further 300 feet along, then came straight back on a parallel run. They reached the end of this run and turned around.

About 100 feet into the third run, John Arland's detector started to flash.

He shouted to Andrew to stop the Rover, then started to clear away dust from what appeared to be a large metal disc.

Julia Brownlow: "This looks artificial, but haven't we been given instructions to ignore anything that looks artificial?"

John Arland: "Well yes, but this is Titanium, and that is one of the metals that we have come to find."

As Andrew and John continued to clear the disc with a brush and with their feet, they noticed a small handle at one side. Andrew took it and pulled it and remarkably he discovered that the disc moved and slid back easily.

John turned on his torch and looked down the hole. He saw steps going down to a different level about thirty feet down.

Andrew: 'I am going down to explore this."

Julia: "I don't know if this is the right thing for us to do,"

John: "I know about that, but I will go down with Andrew, just to take a quick look to see what this is, and where it goes. You can return to the module and wait there and we'll get in contact with you on the radio."

The two descended the steps and started walking, following a winding passage that looked like part of a mine. After a few minutes, John turned to Andrew.

John: "I think we have seen enough, We should go back and take the Rover to the module and report back on what we have seen. We have only an hour of oxygen left".

They turned round and walked back along the passage, but as they approached the hole, still open above them, they were shocked to see the disc slide closed. They ran to the steps, climbed to the disc and tried to open it. But it was locked tight shut.

Andrew: "It's stuck fast. What are we going to do now?"

John: "First we contact Julia and tell her what has happened".

Andrew: "Yes I'll just make it brief and just tell her we are safe."

John called Julia on the radio: "Hello Julia, The disc has closed and it seems to be locked."

Julia: "I know I was standing near the disc and saw it slide shut. I have tried opening it, but it won't move at all."

Andrew: "I am getting the thought that we should go back and see where this passage goes."

John: "That is all we can do and then see if we can find another way out."

They walked back along the horizontal mine shaft and eventually they came to what seemed to be a circular doorway.

John: "Let's see if this will open."

Yet, as they were standing there, the circular door slid back and they saw a space with glass-like walls and a dome-shaped ceiling.

After a pause, a figure approached, about five feet tall, with large dark eyes, a large head and wearing a dark tight-fitting metallic-looking suit. It stepped towards them.

Andrew and John swapped glances. and looked again at the advancing creature.

Andrew spoke first.

Andrew: "We mean no harm. We are explorers from the planet Earth. We want to ask you who you are and why have you brought us here?"

The Being answered through their radio intercom: "First, I want to ask you why you have come here?"

John: "We have been sent here from Earth to seek the possibility of mining for metals and other rare minerals, by the company Halliday Mining Corporation"

The Being asked "And how are you planning to do this?"

John: "It's not up to us how it's going to be done. If the metals are discovered, the company will seek a way to excavate them."

The Being: "It is my task to take you to meet the members of the Council, so please come with me."

They moved off, round a corner, mounted a wheel-less vehicle like a sleigh they moved down the tunnel.

As they travelled, the Being talked to them: "I have a name in our language, and the nearest word in your language is Auron, so you may call me that."

Andrew: "Are you a human?"

Auron: "This body is not biological and it is not mechanical. It is part of both. It is what you might call Android. It has been a long time since I had a biological body. I do not need much oxygen as I have a supply of natural energy."

Andrew: "Who are those people who you are taking us to see?"

Auron: "It is the council who manage the mining in the Moon."

Andrew: "And do they look like you?"

Auron replied, "No, they have human form. I lost my body in an accident, but my mind and my memory have been transferred to this body, that is part biological and part synthetic".

After a few minutes they arrived, leaving the sleigh and went up a passageway, through an airlock and into a beautiful room. Again, it was oval in shape, the wall moulding into the ceiling and it was lit with an imperceptible glow in subtle colours, In the middle there was an oval table with some seats round it.

The astronauts walked into the chamber and moved towards the seating and Auron gestured for them to sit down.

Auron: "It is safe for you to breathe here. You can remove your helmets now."

Moving to an in-built cabinet, Auron picked up several ornamental glasses with some light-yellow liquid in them and indicated that it was safe to drink. They tasted it. It was rich and sweet but not any flavour that they recognised.

After a short wait, a door opened and three men entered and sat down the other side of the table. They were of a dark but Nordic appearance, wearing loose fitting clothes of subtle colours. Speaking in English with a slight trace of accent, one of them stepped forward.

"Greetings and welcome Earth people, My name is Nantes, My concern is the diplomacy and negotiation with other beings who are living in the Universe, primarily with those in our galaxy, that you call the Milky Way.- I would like to introduce you to the other two who are here, this is Rafu, and this Irgon,"

Rafu: "My task is connected with the environment of space, the stars and the planets, you could say the physics, though your science is different to ours."

Irgon: "It is my task to manage issues concerned with the mining on the moon."

"We would like to welcome you to our base on the Moon. I am showing you our way of formal greeting. We do not shake hands in the way that many of your Earth people do. Instead we touch both hands. In this way we can form a circuit and assess whether the individual we are meeting is friendly and relaxed. Do not worry if you are still feeling nervous. This is being done to put you at your ease."

Nantes stepped forward to John and held out his hands and nodded almost imperceptibly. John stepped forward and held out his hands in a similar manner and their fingers touched. John flinched a bit but continued to hold Nantes' fingers, then breathed out in a relaxed manner.

John: "It felt like a current of warm air flowed through my body".

He stepped back and Andrew stepped forward. Nantes and Andrew held out their hands and touched and then stepped back.

Nantes: "Thank you. This is our way of expressing a greeting."

John to Irgon: "So you actually mine the Moon?"

Irgon: "Yes we do it underground using tunnelling. As well as living here on the Moon, we also have large ships that can travel and exist permanently in deep space. We need the materials for maintenance and construction of these ships. Some of this comes from the Moon."

Nantes: "Your Earth people have only recently learned to travel in space but we have been travelling in space for thousands of years. There are many planets where life exists, and when their people develop technology in the way that you are doing, we take more interest, to learn whether they are ready to link up with the community of the galaxy. Currently your rulers are not quite ready to do that."

Irgon: "Our base for mining is the other side of the Moon and is not visible to your telescopes. You call it the dark side. In addition to the Moon, we also have another base on an asteroid that that you call Vesta."

Rafu: "Our science is different from the science in your world. There is no speciality for us. In our culture all science, in fact all study and all beliefs, are all linked up. We see the galaxy as a living organism. We get our power from the life energy that is everywhere in the universe. This is what your people call the aether. We consider this, along with the plasma, to be the atmos or the ambience of space and of the universe. It is the background radiation that is our source of power, also it keeps deep space several degrees above absolute zero in temperature. In space the material, that you call plasma, is magnetic. The planets and the stars and sun are magnetic and some substances, oxygen for example, is magnetic.

"This magnetism creates a flow of natural energy that can run for long distances. When what you call an electrical current starts to flow, it will continue to flow until it is stopped. In space there is nothing to stop it and without any resistance in space these currents may run on for distances of several light years.

"What your people call electricity is the basis of all matter and it is in the nervous systems of all living beings. It is the natural energy holding matter together. Gravity is just another aspect of that electromagnetism.

"Your people have discovered that as one gets closer to the speed of light the mass of objects increases. But by control of gravity, it is possible to create a gravitational field in front of a ship that will pull it through the light barrier and up to the kind of speed that enables crossing the whole galaxy in just a few of your days."

Irgon: "Auron has told us that you have come on an expedition to assess the possibilities of mining on the Moon.

"We have been here on the Moon for many years. Our work is all done below the surface. You may have guessed that from the passage you travelled through on the way here. It is my job to manage the mining in a careful manner."

Nantes leant forward and said: "We know that you have problems of pollution on your planet and we are also concerned about the aggression in your culture. That kind of aggression does not have a place in the Galaxy. We sort out differences through negotiation. The Galaxy has been peaceful for over a thousand years. We are concerned about the number of powerful weapons and bombs and methods of destruction and dissolution that the Governments have in your world. A lot of your culture and entertainment seems to be based on aggression and your vision of space travel seems to be rather violent. We are concerned that if you discover our space travel technology, you may want to bring your weapons and bombs out into space.

"Many years ago, when your people first landed and set their feet on the moon, we thought that your people would be going to recognise and declare our existence. But this never happened. Now you are planning a return to the Moon!

"This means that our presence is more likely to become public knowledge, especially as there are other countries who are also planning to explore the Moon.

"We are not like the primitive natives who can just be driven off, as has happened on Earth many times in your history.

"The governmental, scientific and public recognition of our presence is only a matter of time. Our contact with you and with your corporation means that our presence in the solar system is likely to be recognised and we understand that it will take some time for your culture to change and adapt."

Irgon: "Eventually you will need to report our meeting to your mission control. We do not know yet what the response will be and we hope that you will be safe and secure. We would be prepared to negotiate with your corporation but this will mean the recognition of our existence. We can then work together in collaborating in mining the Moon and possibly other objects in the solar system, for the minerals and metals that you need.

"Earth people have an aggressive culture but, given time, we are hoping that we can come to a peaceful arrangement and that your people can recognise that we are not a threat to you as long as you do not threaten us or attack us. Now you can contact your colleague who is back on the surface, and tell her that you are about to return.

You can pass on the fact that we have had this meeting.

"Auron will now return you to the circular ground hatch that you came through initially, I assume that you will be returning to your landing module and reporting to your mission control. They may decide that you return directly, in which case you will soon rendezvous with your orbiter in preparation to your return to earth."

After the aliens left, the astronauts donned their helmets and returned through the door. Auron led them to the sleigh and they travelled back through the tunnel.

Auron: "The hatch will open as you arrive."

The two left the sleigh. They could see the hatch was opening and they climbed up the stairs. Julia was there, waiting for them.

Julia: "I came back in the Rover to collect you. I reported to Mission Control that you had said that you had met some beings inside the Moon and Mission Control were not too happy about this. They ordered me to collect you and bring you back to the LEM straight away."

They all mounted the Rover and Andrew took over and drove them back to the LEM. Once they were inside the LEM and the hatch was closed they removed their helmets. Two faces came up on the screen. These were Harry and Daniel, the senior mission controllers.

Harry: "I understand that you encountered some beings and it appears that they have an operation beneath the Lunar Surface."

John: "Yes we did."

Harry: "This does have a serious effect on our plans. We will have to ask you all to sign non-disclosure agreements. This must not be allowed to get out. You all understand that, don't you!"

They all nodded.

Daniel: "We have decided to ask you to do one more set of survey runs. Then we will be announcing that the expedition has been a success but due to a minor mechanical problem with the Rover it has resulted in your returning two days early to the Orbiter and then to Earth. You will then be going into isolation on your return. Then we shall arrange a full confidential debriefing."

Back on Earth at Houston, Harry and Daniel were in discussion in the Mission Control office.

Harry: "This is a situation that changes things quite a bit and I would say that as far as the mining project is concerned it is a right old mess."

Daniel: "There was always a risk that something of this nature was going to happen. We can keep it secret for now, but for how long?"

Harry: "Do you think we can continue to do the survey?"

Daniel. "This depends on the aliens. I think we will have somehow to make contact with them and talk to them directly. I don't see how we can go ahead with that unless we inform the higher authority."

Harry: "You mean talk to Halliday himself?"

Daniel: "In this company, that is as high as you can go."

Harry: "It may depend on how it is put to him."

Daniel: "What do you suggest?"

Harry: "The first thing is to inform him that the astronauts have encountered an alien presence on the Moon. Calling him on a confidential video link would be better than a phone call."

Daniel: "I'll do it now."

Daniel picked up the phone.

Secretary: "Mr Halliday's office."

Daniel: "This is Daniel from Mission Control, could you put us through to Mr Halliday?"

Halliday: (on a video link) "Hello."

Daniel: "Mr Halliday, we have something to explain about the Lunar mining project. The Astronauts have encountered an alien presence on the Moon."

Halliday: "How did it happen and what form did it take?"

Daniel: "As they were carrying out the initial survey, they came across what looked like a trapdoor. It was made of Titanium. They were able to open this, and not knowing how old it was they started exploring the tunnel beyond it. After a brief exploration they returned to the exit, but by now it was closed. They had no choice but to explore further down the tunnel. Eventually they came to a closed doorway. They were tapping it and looking for a handle but eventually it opened and an alien being about five foot high, of the 'Grey' type, appeared and questioned them through their radios, in English about their purpose on the Moon."

Halliday: "What happened after that?"

Daniel: "They were taken to a meeting room where they met three more aliens of human form, who explained that they were already mining the Moon.

Halliday: "We will have to bring the astronauts back to Earth and decide on the next move."

CHAPTER 2

The LEM lifted off and linked up with the orbiter and they set course for Earth.

They removed their suits and relaxed.

David: "Space aliens eh? Well it seems something like it was going to happen sometime!"

Andrew: "The way it happened was a surprise for me, but not that much of a surprise that it did happen!"

Julia: "As soon as I saw that titanium slab I thought that things were not quite going to plan!"

John: "We have done all we can. Now it is up to the forces up there and down there!"

As the ship approached the earth, it went into orbit and its surface heated up from the friction with the atmosphere.

Eventually it slowed down and the parachutes went up, the landing legs spread out and the retro-rockets brought it down to earth.

After the landing, they were met by the landing crew and the astronauts were taken into the quarantine truck.

The TV commentator: "The Astronauts have

landed after their return from the Moon, and they will be going into quarantine for two weeks for the medical checks as they have been exposed to dust from the lunar surface."

The commentator turned to the Halliday representative: "What are your comments sir?"

Halliday Representative: "We are really pleased with the way that the mission has turned out and we are planning to send another expedition soon, with a view to proceeding with the mining operation as soon as we can."

Meanwhile Harry spoke to the astronauts over the intercom in the truck.

Harry: "We have been in touch with your wives but only to say that you are feeling well and you hope to be back home soon. No mention of any other experience you may have had until you have all been fully debriefed. The debriefing centre is close to Mission Control. On your arrival you will be required to sign non-disclosure agreements again to cover anything that any of you have seen or heard whilst on the Moon."

The truck took the Astronauts to the Halliday Mission Control in Houston Texas. The astronauts arrived at the debriefing centre and were taken to a large comfortable room with accommodation facilities adjoining. They removed their space suits and put on their casual clothes.

John: "It seems that our sojourn down the tunnel has created a bit of an issue for the people at Mission Control. We will have to wait and see how they cope with it."

Andrew: "I had a hunch that something like this would happen, but to be honest, we did not have much choice."

Julia: "David what do you think about all this?"

David: "I was up in the orbiter and I still don't know a lot about what happened, but it seems like the company are going to try to keep it all under wraps somehow and that puts a lot of pressure on us."

There was a buzz and a screen lit up. Daniel appeared on the screen.

Daniel: "The confidentiality and non-disclosure agreements for you all to sign will be coming from the printer in the room in a few minutes. Tomorrow your quarantine restrictions will be lifted sufficiently for Harry and myself to come over. We need to gather information about these beings that you met and to decide how they might interfere with our plans. Can you tell us what they looked like and how they behaved?"

John: "The first one we met at the end of the tunnel looked like a typical grey specimen, as you might imagine an alien to be, not that tall, spindly legs, fattish face with just nostrils, large bald head, no hair, holes for ears. It explained to us that it lost its body in an accident and that its brain and mind

humanoids who said that they were already mining there."

John: "That's right we have already submitted a report to Harry about it."

Mark: "Yes, I have the report here. It is now more than eighty years since we first landed men on the Moon. An encounter was always likely to happen eventually. Do you think that it would be possible to make contact with them again?"

Andrew: "The Android spoke to us on the radio frequency we were using on the Moon, so we could try that frequency."

Owen: "Good suggestion. We will open that frequency and broadcast toward the moon-every half hour. You gave us their names. Two of them were Irgon and Rafu. We will do that tomorrow. You will return to the Isolation area and we will contact you know if we have any response."

The next day, in the JPL communications room, Owen, and Mark were again with Harry and Daniel, the mission controllers for Halliday Mining.

Owen: "We have the transmitter and receiver open on the relevant channel, with a call going out every 15 minutes, but so far there has been no response."

Harry: "How do you see this going?"

Mark: "Since this expedition was sponsored by Halliday, we are leaving any negotiations to you. NASA is happy to take a back seat at this stage."

Daniel. "None of us have actually met these beings so I suggest that since astronauts John and Andrew are here, we could add their names to the call."

Owen: "I agree. We can have Andrew and John brought over."

A while later, Andrew and John were brought into the room.

Mark: "We have the wavelength that you used on the lunar surface, open. We have had no response so far."

Andrew: "If our voices were put on the call, maybe it would help."

Mark: "I will do that now."

Mark adjusted the equipment and held a microphone to Andrew.

Andrew: "Hello Auron, Nantes, Rafu and Irgun, this is Andrew, I am with John, We met you when we were both inside the Moon and we are hoping to get in contact with you again. If you can get this message, please respond."

They were all sitting there with the message going

out every ten minutes. They heard a crackling sound, then they heard Auron's voice.

Auron: "Yes I can hear you, I am here with Rafu, Nantes and Irgon. We enjoyed your visit and are pleased to be in touch again. Is there any particular message that you wish to bring?"

John: "We are now here at Houston in Texas in the United States on Earth and we are with two people from Halliday and two NASA people."

Rafu: "Do you wish to talk about the mining?"

John: "Not just that. The NASA people want to hear about your culture and the history of the Moon from your point of view."

Rafu, laughing: "We can give you clearer images of that if we could put it on a screen. Here is information about wavelengths and other things."

Mark made adjustments and after a few blips and flashes a portrait image of Rafu appeared.

Rafu: "Can you see me now?"

A chorus of people say "Yes!"

Rafu: "I can see you too. First I will show you some pictures from a different world."

There appeared footage of an elegant city, tower blocks of beautiful organic shapes, almost like a forest of shaped buildings, with pathways winding between them and slow-moving aerial vehicles, some of which passed into the structures through openings that appeared and disappeared as the aerial vehicles passed into them. There were also some humanoid figures walking in the pathways. And there were animals like shorn sheep and small cows. Further away there was a river that expanded into a lake with craft that were oval in shape moving around, and large elegant birds, not unlike swans, that seemed able to take off and land effortlessly. This changed to a rural scene, with a plethora of trees and shrubs but not of a type that anyone recognised. Everyone was mesmerised by these images.

John: "Is this your home planet?"

Rafu: "I can't give you that information just yet. This is for a taste of life on worlds other than your own. The people of the Earth are not yet ready to be invited to enter the Federation of the Galaxy."

Andrew: "It looks very organic, almost as though it all grew there."

The picture returned to Rafu.

Rafu: "Everything there exists on organic principles on the basis of the life energy. The culture exists on a deep level of mutual understanding. The Earth culture is very different to us, It seems in your world you find excuses to release explosive materials onto the dwelling places of impoverished people who have no way of protecting themselves. The search for the truth, that you call religion, in our manner brings people together through a collective experience, In your world it seems to be used as an excuse for conflict and, though I dread to say it, warfare."

During this speech the picture widened to show Nantes and Irgon standing next to Rafu.

Daniel: "What has this got to do with mining?"

Nantes: "If you haven't yet seen it, I will spell it out. The heavy metals and rare earth that you are seeking could be used in creating this terrible weaponry that you seem to be preoccupied with building. This idea does not make us happy; we have no wish to become involved however indirectly in the industry of suffering that your people have created. So, in the short term, we do not support your plan for mining on the Moon."

Harry: "Oh, we would not use it for that purpose, just for peaceful uses, wouldn't we fellas?"

Daniel: "Oh no, we would not use it for weapons manufacture. We have plenty of other needs. There is transport, communication, entertainment and health."

Owen: "We are a peaceful people, we don't want to harm anyone. Take NASA for example, that is a civilian organisation."

Daniel: "We are very pleased to have made contact with you and we would like to get back in contact in the next couple of days. So now we will be signing off."

Nantes: "Goodbye."

Rafu: "Goodbye."

Irgon: "Goodbye."

The screen went blank.

Mark: "An interview with aliens! Well that's a first for JPL!"

Owen: "We said that we wouldn't use any of the minerals for military purposes. I don't think they were convinced."

Harry: "We don't usually ask for a report from our clients, asking them what they planning to use the minerals for."

Andrew: "I think we should stay on friendly terms with them and go back to the Moon. I would like to have a look at these craft that they obviously have."

John: "I agree with that, We should continue trying to negotiate a mining contract and see what they say."

Owen: "The representatives of the JPL and Halliday will have to discuss this tomorrow and then we will get in touch with the astronaut crew members later on and let you know what has been decided."

The next day, Owen and Mark [JPL], with Harry and Daniel of Halliday were present at the meeting in the JPL conference room.

Mark: "We have to move forward on this. I think the points made by John and Andrew are relevant in that we have the opportunity to set up some kind of a deal. And, if necessary, Andrew and John are to be prepared to go back to the Moon."

Owen: "I don't know how you negotiate contracts with these kinds of people, if indeed they are people. We may be facing some sort of a front."

Daniel: "Halliday are used to negotiating contracts. We start with deciding what kind of contract we want and then look at what kind of contract we are likely to get."

Mark: "Well they seem to be pretty much against weapons, so I think we need to make an appeal that is, as far as possible, disconnected from anything military."

Owen: "We really need Halliday to be involved in negotiating this, so if Harry and Daniel could give this consideration, and then let us have an outcome."

Daniel: "The only drawback to that is we may have to give out information to our top managers about the contact that has been made and I am not saying it will, but that it could be a security risk."

Mark: "Just do what you can to ensure confidentiality and come up with your plan."

Harry: "We would initially offer a very modest project and plead poverty on the basis that the Earth's atmosphere has been seriously damaged and that we need rare earth minerals urgently. We need to convert cars, coaches and lorries to electric power."

Mark: "We know nothing about these people, so we might as well try it and see if it works."

Daniel: "It is going to be difficult to draw up a contract without consulting lawyers but the more people that know the harder it will be to keep it secret. I suggest that we work out the wording of a statement and present it to them to see what the reaction is."

Mark: "The four of us could start on that right away."

Daniel: "We need to start with deciding how we are going to address them; we know some names but are they an organisation? Do they have people above them and do they trust us?"

Owen: "Most likely not, since they mentioned weapons."

Harry: "We know that they speak English, so presumably they can also read it and write it."

Daniel: "We can start a message that says Dear Irgon Rafu and Nantes."

Owen: "Do we need to include Auron?"

Harry: "We might as well or they might think we were exclusive."

Daniel: "How about this? To Irgon, Rafu, Nantes and Auron, we appreciate your presence on the Moon and your reasons for being there. The Moon is a satellite of our home planet Earth. We have known it for thousands of years. Our people have landed there and explored it to a modest degree back in the 1970s and we would like to continue to explore it and with agreement from you."

Owen: "Okay so far."

Daniel: "The question of mining has been briefly discussed and we have the impression that there could be some areas where you would permit us to mine in a limited way. We would like to discuss with you where these areas are and how deep we could go, also what you think we might find there."

Owen: "What are they looking for in exchange from us? Would they accept Earth money or resources? I imagine we would be talking about dollars. It would be difficult to fix a price until we had an idea of what the value is, to us, of what we would find would be. How about if we just ask permission to continue to explore and survey a particular area?"

Daniel: "Yes I will include that."

Harry: "I think we should not mention money yet,

just ask permission to go back. I assume that if there is something they want from us, they will make it clear what it is and they will ask for it."

Daniel: So we could just ask permission to survey in the way we were doing before."

Harry: "If we are going to be able to bring back some material, we may need funding from NASA."

Mark: "Because of the different turn this project has taken, NASA would be interested in knowing the extent of the project that the aliens have on the Moon and, from that point of view, could NASA support with funding?"

Owen: "We need to discuss this with the astronauts who will be the ones to return to the Moon, as they have already met the aliens and communicated with them. So will this be the same people? Julia has not met the aliens yet."

Mark: "We will call them all tomorrow and discuss it with them and see if we can make contact again with the aliens."

The following morning a meeting was arranged in the JPL conference room. Present were Mark and Owen from NASA, Harry and Daniel, from Halliday, the three astronauts, John Arland, Andrew Stevenson and Julia Brownlow.

Mark: "We wish to continue to negotiate with the aliens but we do not wish them to think that we are prejudiced against them, so we need to have a term that can use to address them, since they are clearly humanoid. We might refer to them as The Space People. They may want something from us in exchange for what we want from them. Since you, John and Andrew, have contacted them already. We would like to use you for making contact with them again, on a relaxed and not too formal basis."

Owen: "NASA originally made a total of six manned missions to the moon. Since then, in conjunction with Halliday, we are hoping to make further missions in collaboration with the Space People. They do not seem to be opposed to this. John Arland is the senior member of your group and has had negotiating experience, so we will address our remarks to him. But you all have a part to play.

"So John, we would like to arrange a return mission to further explore the resources and you have the responsibility for negotiating an arrangement that would be acceptable to these people. We have no advice to give further than what you have heard discussed. The more that we can find out about the Moon and about them the better. Now that we have reusable space vehicles, the involvement and the expense involved is relatively much less than it was years ago and the flexibility is much greater. All I can say is softly, softly. Are you ready to make a start?"

John: "I will do whatever I can."

Owen: "Are you ready now?"

John: "Yes I am."

Mark turned on the monitor.

John: "Hello Irgun, Nantes, Rafu and Auron, this is John. I am with Andrew. We met inside the Moon and have also had a meeting on this frequency. We are hoping to get in touch with you again. If you can get this message, please come back to us."

They looked at each other and around as the message was repeated a few times.

The monitor flashed and Auron appeared.

Auron: "Yes I can see you and hear you. I am here with Rafu, Nantes and Irgon. We are pleased to be in touch again. Can you tell us the purpose of your call?"

John: "Hello Auron, this is John Arland here. We would like to arrange a return mission to the Moon to further explore the resources and to make an arrangement that would be acceptable to you, the space people. We would like to find out more about the Moon which we think of as our own earth satellite."

Auron: "What did you have in your mind?"

John: "If we were to return to the Moon, could we continue to carry out surveys similar to the two we started, when we found the entrance to your base?

We would also like to do a survey of the Moon, as far as we can."

Auron: "That is the concern of Irgon and I will turn the screen to him."

Irgon: "What equipment will you be bringing? Is this the same as before?"

John: "Initially yes."

Irgon "Are you planning to use drilling equipment?"

John: "Our company would like to."

Irgon: "And how would this be powered?

John: "I don't know if the company has made a decision on that."

Irgon: "We have a hunch that they are planning to use nuclear power."

John: "I really don't know."

Irgon: "That nuclear energy you use is dangerous and it produces a lot of contaminated waste that lasts for thousands of years, so would you tell your company that we do not want any equipment on the Moon that produces nuclear radiation."

John: "Oh, if they did use it they would take all the waste back to earth none would be left on the Moon!"

Irgon: "It is not just that. For us the very presence of your kind of nuclear equipment is contaminating. You will have to use something else, to find another way."

John, "So would solar panels be acceptable?"

Irgon: "Power from the sun would be agreeable, as you use in your earth satellites, that would be acceptable to us."

John: "Where do you want us to search?"

Irgon: "We have given this some thought and there is an area near the North Pole of the Moon we will permit you to examine but you must not go too deep."

John: "What do you call deep?"

Irgon: "In your measurements two hundred feet."

John: "That does not sound very deep."

Irgon: "Much of the Moon is hollow. If you go too deep your people and their equipment could fall through into a chasm and that would be very dangerous for you and for us as well. For that reason there must be close co-operation between you and us during your operations."

John: "Thank you Irgon, for the information you have given us. We look forward to having details of the part that you will permit us to explore. You have not yet met Julia Brownlow, she is our expert in surveying and navigation, and I am expecting her to be present at our next meeting. Thank you and your friends. We will now be signing off."

Irgon: "Us as well."

The screen went blank.

Mark: "That was a good start, so thank you John."

Owen: "The limitations they have set do not surprise us. But this indicates that at this stage it should be regarded as an exploratory project rather than a commercial one. I will be passing on details to Peter Bridgewater the Chief NASA administrator, regarding funding for further expeditions and the CIA space department may have to be informed regarding security aspects."

Harry: "The next communication with the Moon people will need to include Julia with regard to surveying and mapping of the landing area. So, if we reconvene next week, we can report on progress then and discuss ways of taking it forward."

A week later there was another meeting in the JPL conference room.

Present were Mark and Owen from NASA, Harry and Daniel from Halliday, and the three astronauts, John Arland, Andrew Stevenson and Julia Brownlow.

Daniel: "I have been in touch with members of the Board of Halliday who assured me that the Company are committed to the project and they will be planning a further stage in the Moon project in the next two months, subject to further information regarding the choice of a landing site and survey area."

Harry: "We are hoping to make contact with the space people again to report this and find out if there has been developments their end."

Mark: "Okay with us. I will set up the wavelength for you to use."

Harry: "We would like John to carry out the first contact to maintain consistency."

Mark switched on the equipment and some background noise was heard.

John: "Hello Auron. This is John Arland. We have been in contact with authorities both at Halliday and at NASA and have secured agreement to arrange a return mission to the Moon along the lines we discussed last week."

This message was repeated several times, while the assembled group patiently waited.

After a while Auron's face appeared on the monitor screen.

Auron: "Hello Earth people. We thank you for contacting us again."

John: "Hello Auron. This is John Arland. We have been in contact with authorities both at Halliday and at NASA and have got agreement to arrange a return mission to the Moon on the lines we discussed last week."

Auron: "Yes we understand that."

John: "We wondered if there had been any developments at your end."

Auron: "We have been in further contact with official people on our side who have expressed a desire to meet with your people to further discuss arrangements before any excavation is carried out. This could include an examination of the site and some of the facilities that we have on the Moon."

John: "Our team would include our expert in surveying and navigation, Julia Brownlow, as I mentioned in our previous meeting."

Auron: "Meeting her would be suitable for us. If we are informed of your expected date and time for your next arrival. We will give you a suitable landing location. There will be a negotiation before any activity on the surface. We wait to see and hear you on this matter."

John: "Thank you Auron. We are signing off now."

The screen went blank.

CHAPTER 3

In the editorial office of the National Investigator, Edward, the editor was allocating stories to the staff, several journalists were present.

Editor: "Richard, I want you to report on the National Football League final. Sandra, I want you to cover the celebrity fashion show, the one that is being done for charity. Jane, I want you to look into this mining on the moon story. The expedition came back earlier than expected and we were told that there had been a malfunction on the Moon Rover. This company Halliday is planning to excavate rare metals on the moon, and they can't supply a Rover that does not break down on the first trip out. There could be something happening on the moon that we have not been told about, I suspect a little bit of what shall I say, a cover- up? So Jane, I'd like you to dig around and see what you can find."

Jane Westgate: "Yes I can see what you are getting at, I will make some enquiries, I'll start with Halliday."

Jane Westgate returned to her office and turned on her computer and looked at a webpage. She picked up the phone and dialled a number.

Jane: "Hello I'm Jane Westgate from the National Investigator. I would like to talk to someone about these mining expeditions on the Moon."

Receptionist: "Yes I'll put you through to someone who can help."

There was a long wait and then a voice came on the phone.

Voice: "How can I help you?"

Jane: "I'd like to get some information about Halliday's mining project on the Moon."

Voice: "It's all going ahead as normal."

Jane: "It doesn't sound very normal to me, what with the Moon Rover breaking down. Was it the Moon Rover breaking down again on the second expedition too?"

Voice: "The Moon Rover worked normally."

Jane: "There is a rumour going round that there are aliens on the Moon!"

Voice: "I'll get back to you on that. Goodbye."

The voice ended the call.

Jane placed the phone down, looked puzzled, then picked up the phone again and dialled another number, this time to the editor's office.

Jane: "You'll never believe what happened when I

phoned up Halliday and asked for some information about the mining expedition. I was put through to a voice who said everything was going ahead as normal. So I then said that there is a rumour that there are aliens on the Moon and he just said I'll get back to you and rang off!!"

Editor: "Is that all he said?"

Jane: "He actually said I'll get back to you on that, goodbye, and rang off.

"So whoever it was hasn't got back to me yet, but what does it mean?

"Does it mean that there are aliens on the Moon? Like you said, there is something fishy here and I'd like to be the one to catch it. He didn't say who he was so I don't know who to ask for."

Editor: "If you ring back, you'll probably get a denial. Anyhow, it sounds like a good strong story, so keep in touch."

Jane:, "Don't worry I will, Byee!"

Jane (to herself): "I need to talk to some UFO buffs, to see what they say."

Scanning through pages in the internet, Jane found one called UFO College. She decided to give them a call.

"Hello…"

"Hello, "I am Jane Westgate and I am a reporter

looking into issues around unidentified aerial phenomena and I am hoping you can help me."

Arnold Hope: "That's what we are here for. My name is Arnold Hope. What particular aspect are you interested in?"

Jane: "It's to do with the Halliday Moon mission. There are things that don't tie up about these missions and I think it might be to do with aliens. I am hoping that you might give me some background."

Arnold: "Well I can tell you about some recent developments. A short while ago UFOs were big news, and media outlets like The New York Times and 60 Minutes were running stories on shadowy objects that appeared to dart and dance in grainy video clips that had been taken by Navy jet pilots. Last June though, the Pentagon issued a report on nearly two decades' worth of the unidentified aerial phenomena or UAP, the government's preferred new term for UFOs. It suggested that the objects could be drones, weather-related phenomena or just glitches on a screen.

"On the other hand, in some cases, these objects appear to exhibit unusual flight characteristics. And meanwhile, a recent Pew Research Centre poll has found that more than half of Americans believe that it's aliens that are steering the UFOs.

"One of the problems is that many of the areas where we're seeing the greatest level of UFO activity are restricted military airspace. The

Defence Department are not excited about the idea of us bringing along instruments to record everything that's going on.

"Anyhow, why don't you come up and see us and stay at the UFO College for a few days? We have a festival next week, with discussions, lectures, films, and not just about UFOS, we also deal with yoga, astrology, astronomy and Tai Chi.

"There's even a group coming here that reveres the whole Universe as a living organism. They claim that there is an energy of life that flows throughout the universe that science has not yet discovered.

"And you could do us a favour by helping in relations with the local people."

Jane: "All sounds fascinating. Where is the College?"

Arnold: "It's in Maine."

Jane: "Oh I hadn't thought it was that far. I'll have to ask my boss. I'll be seeing him tomorrow."

Next morning, Jane called in at the editor's office.

Jane: "Morning Edward. I've been in contact with this organisation called UFO College in Maine and they have a gathering next week. They have discussions, with lectures and films, not just about UFOS, they deal with yoga, astrology, astronomy and Tai Chi.

"They have invited me up there to stay for a few days."

Editor: "That sounds good, would you like to go?"

Jane: "Well It would fill me in on a lot of aspects of this subject that I am not that familiar with or clear about. Also, I wondered whether you wanted me to try and get an interview with an astronaut?"

Editor: "I have been looking into that, and they have all signed confidentiality agreements. I don't think the company would be happy about one of our staff nosing around and trying to get them to break those agreements. However, this UFO college sounds interesting. Do they charge?"

Jane: "Normally, yes, but they have asked me to do some public relations with the local community in exchange for the board."

Editor: "Well you could write us a column about your experiences on some of the lecture subjects. I'll book you a flight."

Jane arrived at Portland Airport and took a taxi to the UFO college. From there she could see a field with tents and tepees, cars and caravans. There was a large geodesic dome shaped marquee and several other smaller domes, with a large grassed area marked out by tall poles with pennants fluttering on their tops. There was a house with an office building adjacent to it. Jane walked to the office carrying her case. She entered the office and spoke to the young lady sitting behind a table.

Jane: "Hello, I am Jane Westgate and I have been booked in by Arnold Hope."

Receptionist: "Ah yes, he's in the house, I'll let him know you are here."

Jane entered the house and met Arnold. He was a dark slim studious-looking type.

Arnold: "Hello Jane, glad you could make it. I'll show you to your room."

Upstairs, he showed her into a room that has a single bed, a chair and a cupboard.

Arnold: "The toilet is just down the corridor. There is a cafe in a tent in the field. I am busy for the moment but we can have a chat later."

After a while, Jane walked to the field. Many of the tents had patterns painted on them. She could see several smaller geodesic domes around the site and there was a marquee with a sign over it saying Café. In the distance she could see what looked like a mobile shower unit with a row of toilets nearby. She approached the big geodesic dome. It contained rows of chairs and she assumed it to be like a lecture hall. Near the entrance there was a list of the day's events, some of which were marked as being workshops in the smaller domes. Then she went into the Café marquee, bought a cup of tea and a sandwich and picked up a leaflet listing the day's events.

She could see during that afternoon in the Big Dome there was to be a talk entitled The Living Energy Around Us And In Space.

At the allotted time, Jane entered the Dome and sat down, waiting for the talk to begin.

After a few minutes, the speaker entered and addressed the audience from a small stage in front of a screen.

Speaker: "Most people think of electricity as the stuff that heats the water when you boil a kettle, or that lights a bulb when you turn on a switch, but electricity is so much more than that. The electron is very versatile. It is in every substance, and can float around in space on its own in which case it carries an electric charge.

"When you look up at the sky, what do you see? Most days you can see the clouds. Those clouds are of tons of water, but how does it stay up there? The answer is that an electrical charge holds the molecules of water attached to the molecules of oxygen and nitrogen that constitute the atmosphere.

"Electrons are miniscule but every atom of matter has many of them. Sometimes they behave as particles and sometimes they behave as waves. How many each atom has determines on what the substance is. Each atom of oxygen, for example, has eight electrons whereas an atom of lead has eighty-two.

"The nervous system of animals, including humans, contain electricity and it was through animals, specifically frogs, that electricity as we know it was first discovered. When atoms and molecules have the correct number of electrons there is no overall charge, but if the atoms have lost electrons or have too many electrons attached to them then there is an electrical charge.

"There are two kinds of electrical charge, positive and negative. Too few electrons give a positive charge, too many electrons give a negative charge. This is how atoms bond to form molecules. For example two atoms of hydrogen bond with one atom of oxygen to form the water molecule, H_2O. The more atoms that bond together make more complex molecules. So it is electric charge that is the basis of all matter and all life.

"Benjamin Franklin, the American writer and politician, in the eighteenth century experimented with electricity. He was concerned about buildings in the fledgling America that were being damaged by lighting. It was his theory that lightning was electrical. To test this theory, he flew a kite in a thunderstorm and was able to catch electrical charge from the cord connected to the kite into a Leyden Jar, an early form of electricity storage. He established that lightning was electric and that electricity has two charges,

"For Franklin, the electricity coming down from the sky was a negative force, because it damaged buildings. So he named it a negative pole. We now know that it is the flow of electrons that makes electricity, but it is still referred to as the negative charge. From this, Franklin also invented the lightning conductor.

"Out in space there's a lot of material, dust and so on, that is either negatively or positively charged. This has been called plasma.

"Similar charges repel each other and opposite charges attract each other. Gravity moves the clouds of this charged material in space, this creates magnetic fields and this produces electric currents. Magnetism itself had been detected in space by probes since the 1970s.

"It was Albert Einstein who established the existence of the electron as a particle of electricity. He also discovered that light was made up of particles now called photons. He was awarded a Nobel prize for these discoveries.

"It has since been established that both light and electricity behave both as waves and also as particles. Light has been referred to as light waves for generations; so if light is a wave, then it must be a wave in a medium. The existence of such a medium was recognised In the eighteenth century and called the aether.

"However, in his general relativity theory Einstein did not mention aether. Instead, he put forward a theory that gravity is a geometric property of space and time. In this case it would be fair to claim that the aether is also a property of space and possibly of time.

"Einstein's theory of gravity is either incorrect or at least incomplete. Einstein's theory of general relativity and gravitation was published in 1915. There have been no further developments in the discovering the nature of gravity in more than a hundred years since then. A lot of people feel that it is the scientific establishment's obsession with Einstein's theory that has held up scientific development in this area for over a hundred years."

"In the 1940s and 50s, there was a psychoanalyst named Wilhelm Reich who as well as working in psychotherapy was studying the behaviour of microbes. He found there was a field of energy around microbes and, when he tried to isolate it, he found it was everywhere in the atmosphere. He called it Orgone. At the time, Reich's books were available in most bookshops. He used his discoveries for healing and even for influencing the weather.

"In the early days of the cold war, unfortunately Reich became involved in politics. He wrote to the authorities claiming that he could treat radiation sickness with Orgone. He was then charged with fraud and jailed. He died in prison.

"Recently, a movement has arisen that claims that it is not just gravity that controls the bodies in space but that, out there, electricity has a major part to play. This is called the electric universe theory and I will be talking more about that later in the week."

At the end of the talk, the speaker offered to answer questions.

A question was asked about electric eels.

Speaker: "The first fish that were known to have electric qualities were in the river Nile that runs through Egypt. They were called torpedo fish, and were used for healing. However, the electric eels in the Amazon river are much more powerful and can create a sting of two hundred volts, that can be fatal. This shows how powerful animal electricity can be."

After the talk, Jane went back to her room and settled down for the evening thinking about what she had heard In the talk.

The following morning, Jane took a walk in the pine forest surrounding the site, looking at the trees and listening to the birds. After taking lunch, she returned to the dome marquee to hear another talk, this one entitled The Day a Flying Saucer Crashed Near the Town of Roswell.

She sat down and another speaker stepped onto the stage.
Speaker: "It was the evening of July 4th 1947, while the country was celebrating Independence Day, that the radar operators in the control tower at the Roswell U S Army Air Force base were watching the strange blip that turned up again and again on their screens, pulsating, glowing more intensely and then dimly. At the same time as this, there was a tremendous thunderstorm that was breaking out over the desert.

"The operatives in the control tower had never seen a blip behaving like this, as it darted across the screen at speeds that would have been well over a thousand miles an hour. All the while it was pulsating, and throbbing. Then the blip passed to the lower quadrant of the screen. For a moment, it seemed to disappear. Then in an explosion of brilliant white fluorescence the blip evaporated and the screen was clear. The blip had gone.

"Controllers looked around at each other and at the CIC officers in the room, the same thought arose in all their minds. The object, whatever it was, had crashed!

"At around that time, rancher Matt Pretzel was in his ranch house with his two young kids, when a terrible storm blew up. It was the worst storm he had ever seen, not much rain, but lightning, strike after strike. In the middle of the storm there was an explosion, that was different from a lightning strike.

"The next morning, Matt Pretzel was riding out over the pasture to check some sheep, when he came across wreckage spread over a strip of land and stretching for about four hundred yards. It was wreckage like he had never seen before. He collected some up, and he was persuaded to take it along to Roswell Air base where they detained him for a several hours and then made him promise not to tell anyone about it."

Speaker: "The craft itself was discovered in a desert area by a group of archaeologists searching for ancient Indian artefacts. They found that one side of the craft was split open and they could see inside. There were two creatures about four foot tall, one of which was in a sitting position at what appeared to be a control desk. There were also other bodies that were lying around. Several other people arrived and witnessed the scene.

pater in the morning, the military arrived, and cordoned it off. The disk and the bodies were collected and finally transported to an air force base in California.

"Engineers at Edwards Air Force Base examined the craft and could find no engine or fuel so it was assumed by them that somehow the craft had turned electromagnetism into anti-gravity.

The speaker then delved into a bag and took out what looked like an old newspaper cutting.

Speaker: "On July the eighth 1947, the Roswell Daily Record local newspaper, carried the headline 'USAAF Captures Flying saucer in the Roswell Region'.

"The report went on, 'The intelligence office of the eighth Bombardment group of the Roswell Army airfield, announced at noon today that the field has come into possession of a flying saucer. According to information released by the authority of Major Jesse Marcel the base intelligence officer, the disc was collected from a ranch in the Roswell vicinity after a rancher had notified Sheriff George Wilcox that he had found the instrument on his premises. Major Marcel and a detail went to the ranch and recovered the disc, it was stated. After intelligence officers had inspected the disc, it was transported to headquarters."

The speaker put down the sheet he was reading and looked round at the audience.

Speaker: "Later press reports denied the story, claiming that it was a weather balloon."

"Many years later in 1960, Colonel Philip Corso, who was the officer in charge of the foreign technology desk, was sitting at the desk in his office at the Pentagon. If any technical equipment

from fo͜ʲn countries came into the hands of the
militaʳ was passed on to him and it was his
task͜xamine it and to pass it on to any
coɲ that was researching in that area.

day, he was looking through the contents
"͜ that had been brought into his office. He
͜ived an instruction that he should write a
ɲ its contents. He opened it up and looked
There was nothing that he recognised. It
ɩ to be a jumble of technological
ent. He walked down the corridor to the
ɩf his boss, General Harrow. He asked him
he delivery. All the General said was to find
ɲat you can about the Roswell incident.

orso returned to his office and looked again at
ɲe material. Things began to fall into place in his
mind. He had heard of the Roswell incident and
realised that this material was from the wreckage
that had been gathered up by the army at the time.
Most likely it had all since been packed away
because the army had not known what to do with
it. There was material there in the delivery case
that could be relevant to lasers, fibre optics, night
visions, printed circuitry and many other things.
Corso was given instructions to visit companies
researching and working in those areas, wearing
civilian clothes and to pass on any relevant
information, without giving any indication that it
had a military connection."

The speaker ended his talk without giving any

opportunities for questions.

After the talk, Jane went back to her r
consider the significance of what she had he o

CHAPTER 4

The following morning, Jane went down to have breakfast and meet with Arnold Hope who had invited her to have breakfast with him.

Arnold: "What do you think about what you have heard so far?"

Jane: "Well it's a lot to take in, the idea that Einstein's theory of general relativity has delayed gravity research, and that developments in electronics might have come from an alien spaceship are astonishing!"

Arnold: "There were several people who worked on anti-gravity experiments in the 1930s such as Paul Biefield and Townsend Brown, but none of those have been followed up, at least not publicly."

Jane: "Why do you think that the authorities are so keen to deny the existence of UFOs and space people, when they have so much evidence of their existence?"

Arnold: "Well the reason that is often quoted is that the War of the Worlds broadcast made by Orson Wells in the 1930s, caused riots, because people thought it was a real space invasion. But that is not the real reason."

Jane: "Yes, there must be more to it than that."

Arnold: "After the newspaper report about the Roswell crash went round the world, the intelligence services went into overdrive to cover things up. The Military assume that they are hostile and, since they have no defence against them, the rather unconvincing weather balloon story came about.

"Look at it this way. In 1947, the US military was the most powerful in the world. They had just used a nuclear weapon to effectively end the biggest war the world had ever seen. They did not want to become side-lined into being residents on a minor planet on the outskirts of the Galaxy that was ruled by heaven knows who? Anyone who was even claiming to have seen a UFO was regarded as a security risk. Something of that attitude still exists."

Jane: "Why do you think it was that the last Apollo Moon missions were never completed?"

Arnold: "The official reason was budgetary, to save money, but that is unlikely to have been the real reason, because the money had already been spent. The rockets and equipment were already to go. One Apollo rocket was subsequently used to launch the Skylab space station and the other two are on display at Houston, as museum exhibits. I can't tell you exactly but, thinking back to the 1970s, twenty Moon landings had been planned, but Apollo 17 was the last one that was carried out. The last three were cancelled.

"After Neil Armstrong made his speech about one small step for a man and a giant leap for mankind, he then went on to say that they're watching us from the ridge. He had seen a craft in the distance. But of course, that was not broadcast.

"Another thing was that there were ten manned Gemini orbital space missions in preparation for the Moon landing. The Gemini was a capsule, not unlike the Mercury capsule, only bigger, as it carried two astronauts and it could stay in space for longer. Anyhow, several of the Gemini missions were tracked by alien space vehicles."

Jane: "I never heard that."

Arnold: "The Apollo 17 mission went to an area of particular interest and one or two of the comments that the astronauts made have never been explained. There was a new President and there were disturbances back on earth, riots and so forth, so the authorities may have decided that they had done enough and seen enough. They had claimed that they could do things the Russians couldn't do, so let's pack up now and call it a day."

Jane: "You mean contacts they didn't want to make?"
Arnold "That's right, there is a rumour that the Aliens have a base on the Moon, but nothing has

been proved."

Jane: "That's very interesting, I was asked by my editor to find out why the Halliday Moon mining project had gone quiet. So I called up Halliday and when I asked them to put me through to someone I could ask about the Moon mining project. They put me through to someone, I don't know his name, but when I suggested that their team could have met aliens on the Moon, he didn't deny or affirm this, he just said that he would ring me back. But I haven't heard any more from him."

Arnold: "Well, of course it's quite possible that they did."

Jane: "I came along here to get some background about the situation."

Arnold: "Well, let us know if there is anything more that we can do to help. I can give you a contact number for Franco Savarez. He has quite an active group down your way and it might well be worth your while contacting him."

Jane: "Thank you for that. Meantime I need to get back and report to my boss, and to see if there have been any more developments at his end."

Jane took a taxi to the airport and boarded the plane back to Houston. In the morning she went in to the offices of the National Investigator.

Jane: "Morning Boss.

Editor: "How did it go?"

Jane: "Well I went to a talk about the living energy that flows round the universe, and another about a saucer that crashed in Roswell in 1947. I had an interesting chat with Arnold Hope about the Apollo missions, and why they didn't run the last three missions. He thinks that it was because they were starting to find things that they did not want to find."

Editor: "There could be something in that. In the Halliday Mining missions, it is also quite possible that they are finding things they do not want to find, as well. And if that is so, we need to look into what they are."

Jane: "Well it can only be to do with space people, can't it? In the talk about the Roswell incident, it was also explained how a Colonel Corso was investigating these wafer-like little plates. He took them to Fell Electronics who were doing research in that area. The chief scientist said yes we know about these because we had access to the ship soon after the crash. We used that technology to develop transistors and integrated circuits."

Editor: "Can you write a piece for the Investigator about what you have found out?"

Jane: "Will do, When we have finished here, I'll get

on to it straight away."

Jane went back to her flat and made a cup of coffee. She walked into the sitting room, sat down on the settee, and sipped the coffee. Then she took a notebook out of her handbag and looked up a number. She picked up the phone and dialled it.

Jane: "Hello. Is that Franco Savarez?"

Savarez: "Speaking."

Jane: "I was given your contact details by Arnold Hope at the UFO College He suggested I get in touch."

Savarez: "Oh yeah? Well if you're interested, our group has a meeting tomorrow night. Would you like to come along?"

Jane: "That would be good. Please let me have the details and I'll be there."

Sav's UFO group met in the function room behind a café. Jane entered and saw that there were about twenty people there, some older and some looked like the people she had seen and met at the UFO College. Savarez was about to open and address the group.

Savarez: "Evening everybody, I'd like you to meet Jane Westgate."
Jane, sitting near the front, stood up and took a

little bow of acknowledgement and sat down again.

Savarez: "On account of Jane's interest in the subject, tonight we are going to discuss what we think might have happened to the Halliday Moon expedition. Anyone got any ideas?"

Various audience members stood in sequence and made comments.

Brian: "I think there are giant worms on the Moon who came out their holes and threatened to eat up the astronauts."

Matthew: "Can we be sure that they ever went to the Moon anyway?"

Veronica: "I think the Moon is hollow and they found out that if they started mining, they could fall through the hole and wind up floating about in the giant space inside the Moon and wouldn't be able to get out."

Ian: "Maybe there is radiation on or around the Moon and they were worried they might get radiated."

Savarez: "Jane, what do you think?"

Jane: "I've enjoyed hearing all your interesting theories. I was hoping that coming back to Houston, someone might have heard something, a rumour or anything from anyone connected with Halliday or with the astronauts."

Muriel: "I know someone who knows the wife of one of the Astronauts and she said that although they are not supposed to talk about it, she has hinted that her husband did meet aliens on the Moon."

Jane: "Any indication what they looked like? Were they human or more like the greys?"

Muriel: "Apparently there were both types, I can't say any more than that."

The following morning, Jane was back in her flat next morning and making breakfast when the phone rang.

Jane: "Oh hello Franco."

Savarez: "What did you think of the meeting?"

Jane: "I enjoyed it and glad I came along. What that lady Muriel said was really interesting, that a friend of hers heard it said by the wife of one of the crew. It was a pity she couldn't give us any more information."

Savarez: "Yes it was. However, I didn't mention this last night at the meeting but I am also In touch with a hacker. He has hacked into the lines of some Halliday employees and also into the line of NASA."

Jane; "Oh really, There must be some interesting stuff there."

Savarez: "There is. He is not very far away, the best thing would be for us to go over there and meet him. We could do that this afternoon."

Jane: "That sounds good."

Savarez: "How about I see you outside the café where we had the meeting, at half past two, and I'll take you over there in the car."

Jane met Savarez, went outside the cafe and they set off in his car. They pulled up outside a sophisticated log cabin and approached the door and Franco knocked. The door was answered by a swarthy man of medium build.

Savarez: "Roy this is Jane, who I mentioned to you on the phone."

Jane: "Hello Roy."

Roy: "Come in"

They entered and went through to the sitting room.

Roy: "Coffee?"

Savarez nodded.
Jane: "Yes please."

Roy: "Franco has mentioned that you are interested in the Halliday Moon expedition. I have been able to hack into the phones of some of the Halliday staff.

"They are upset about all this secrecy and with the way that the whole business is being handled. They know that the astronauts encountered aliens on the Moon. They met one grey and three of human type.

"However, there are Halliday staff who think the whole situation should be made public, especially since the Company paid for the trip.

"There is a global network of UFO groups who are following this closely and so, in that sense, the secret is already out.

"As I am in contact with you Franco, I will let you know If we can get a bit further ahead with this and I will deal with this matter through you."

Savarez: "Thank you Roy. We will have to get back now as I have some other business to attend to."

Savarez and Jane moved towards the door and said goodbye.

Savarez and Jane got back in the car.

Jane: "Did you know about this already?"

Savarez: "Some of it yes, but things are now moving on quickly."

Savarez dropped her off at her flat and they said goodbye.

A few days later, Jane was working in her flat when the phone rang.

Savarez: "Hello Jane, its Franco, I've had a call from Roy. Are you free today? If so, I'll pick you up at two o'clock."

Jane: "Yes, that's fine."

Savarez pulled up outside her flat and she got into the car. They drove to Roy's ranch-house.

Roy let them in. They sat down in the sitting room.
Roy: "I have some further information to confirm about how the Halliday astronauts made contact with the aliens. They were exploring a tunnel and it led to a door and as they were examining it, it opened and, there they met Auron the Android, who asked them why they were there. They explained that they were on a mission to explore the possibilities of mining on the Moon. Apparently they were taken on a vehicle through

another tunnel and to an oval room with tables and seating. There they met the three human-type aliens whose names were Irgon, Rafu and Nantes. This was when it was explained to them that the aliens were already mining on the Moon!"

CHAPTER 5

One week later, there was another meeting in the JPL conference room. Again present were Mark and Owen from NASA, Harry and Daniel from Halliday, and the three astronauts, John Arland, Andrew Stevenson and Julia Brownlow.

Mark: "I understand that agreement has been made for the target time for the next launch. The next Moon landing is three weeks' time. You have all been briefed on this but we need to talk to the space people to discuss their suggested Moon landing site. We also have some suggested landing sites. Since you are all here, I will set up a signal to contact Auron and the space people."

Mark turned on the transmitter and receiver and nodded to John to start the message.

John: "Hello Auron, John Arland here, we have a possible return date for three weeks' time and look forward to your proposal for a landing site."

After a few minutes, Auron's voice was heard.

Auron: "Hello Earth people. We suggest that your landing point is in the north west corner of the area that you call the Mare Imbrium. We can then direct you on your Moon Rover to the access point. The day you mentioned in three weeks' time is suitable. There is an access point just under three of your earth miles north-east of the landing point. It will open when you arrive and I will be there to take you to the Negotiation Hall."

Three weeks later, the astronauts prepared to return to the Moon.

The astronaut team was as before, Andrew Stevenson, John Arland, Julia Brownlow and the orbiter pilot, David Jones.

On the appointed day, the team mounted and ascended to the ship, and take-off proceeded as normal. After the two-day voyage to the Moon, Andrew guided the ship safely down to the designated landing site and John sent out a call signal to Auron.

John: "Hello Auron, this is John. We have landed and are unloading the Rover. As soon as we are ready, we will head out north west as directed."

Auron: "Hello John and your crew. Take it slowly as the surface is uneven. You will find a path that runs over the crater and beyond that is the access point."

Andrew drove steadily and Julia looked around to survey the jagged landscape.

John had a telescopic electronic viewer and was scanning to find the pathway that Auron had mentioned.

John: "I think I can see it, slightly to the right of where we are heading."

Julia: "Can I have a look, John?"

John handed the viewer to Julia.

Julia: "Oh yes, I have it now. It is quite smooth and it does look like it has been artificially cleared. It is narrower than I would have expected and it looks quite steep. Take it carefully Andrew!"

By now they were approaching the track and Andrew reduced speed further. They approached the brow of the hill and as they crossed over the peak, they could see that the track running alongside an area that included what seemed to be a flat disc. It looked quite similar to the one they originally entered on their first Moon landing but larger in diameter.

They pulled up and stopped alongside it and walked out around the disc.

Then they heard Auron's voice on the radio.

Auron: "When the access point opens, you can enter down the steps and I will meet you there."

The hatch slid open and they saw a stairway, more elaborate than the one before and it went deeper. In single file they descended the stairway, Auron was at the bottom to greet them.

He was standing by the door of a cylindrical vehicle that was larger than the one they had previously ravelled in. It was enclosed with elegantly upholstered seating.

Andrew examined the vehicle. It was a matt silver colour with a rounded nose. He could not see any wheels or propulsion unit. It seemed to be floating just above the track. Down, the tunnel that looked like a narrow path. They settled into the seating.

Auron touched a keyboard beside him and they set off silently but with an acceleration that they could feel.

Auron: "Welcome back to the satellite that you call your Moon, we will be arriving at the Negotiation Hall in a few of your Earth minutes."

John: "Auron I would like you to meet Julia. She is our navigation and surveying expert."

Auron: "Welcome Julia."

Julia: "Pleased to meet you Auron."

Still in their spacesuits, as the vehicle gently accelerated, they could feel themselves getting lighter and they put their hands down to hold the metal loops beside their seats to prevent themselves from floating off.

Andrew: "The gravity is getting less and this is caused as we are getting closer to the centre of the Moon."

Auron: "Partly that, also the acceleration. The gravity will steadily return as we approach the landing stage for the Negotiation Hall."

They could feel the gravity returning and then, as the vehicle slowed down, they could see a platform as the craft came to a halt. It was not dissimilar to a subway station but more elegant and colourful.

Auron led them down the passageway and within five minutes they came to an airlock that opened. Beyond was an entrance to a great and beautiful oval shaped hall, radiant in elegant organic flowing patterns. Irgon, Nantes and Rafu were standing ready to meet them.

Rafu: "Welcome back, friends. Auron will lead you to the changing room where you can remove your suits and where there are some comfortable clothes and robes that you are most welcome to use if you wish.

John: "Thank you, that would be most welcome. We will change, and then come back for the formalities."

Auron led them to the changing room where they found an array of loose-fitting trousers, robes and jackets. Attached to the changing room was a toilet, not unlike those on the Earth.

The three chose from the available garments and returned to the Hall. Irgon, Rafu and Nantes were waiting there for them. They held their hands forward to touch the hands of the astronauts in turn, as a formal greeting.

Nantes: "We have a visitor from our home planet who has travelled here to meet you and to establish connection with the people of the Earth. If you sit down and make yourself comfortable, Auron will serve you with refreshment. She is an ambassador from our home solar system and it is her task to investigate whether our civilisations can interact. I'll not say any more, please stand when she enters."

Gentle sounds of music seemed to fill the air, the lighting subtly changing as the doors opened.

A tall elegant lady with shoulder length flowing hair and wearing a colourful ankle length robe entered.

Everyone was standing in a line. First the space people, then the astronauts, John, Andrew and Julia, with Auron at the end of the line. The lady walked up to each one, held out her hands and their fingers on both hands touched, as they had done with the space people in the previous visit. It was done in a subtle manner and they felt a warm response. She gestured for them to sit down and then sat down herself in a throne-like chair slightly higher than the others.

Nantes: "I would like to introduce you all to Maralina, the Deputy Ambassador of our home planetary system."

Maralina: "We are hoping that our meeting can eventually lead to a constructive outcome between our civilisations. We have had contact in the distant past with cultures on the Earth, in Africa, North and South America, India and Australia.

"We understand that you have come to explore the prospect for mining on the Moon, but without having the awareness that the Moon is already being mined.

"First though, I would like to explain something of the science and philosophy of our civilisation. For us, the whole universe is living and intelligent, in the sense that there is a radiation of living energy everywhere.

"Whereas your space stations use light from the sun as the power source, we can use the radiation that is everywhere for our power.

"As a result of the flow of currents that you call electricity, this comes about as a result of natural magnetism.

"By understanding and using gravity, our craft can travel through space, in the vicinity of the gravity of planets and even through what you call the light barrier.

"There was no 'Big Bang' in the way that your scientists claim. The universe is eternally regenerating through the natural energy that flows everywhere.

"The environment of space and deep space is very sensitive. This is where stars, planets and moons, comets and asteroids are born. Chemical reactions can occur in space.

"To give an example, water is created in space as a result of the bonding of synthesised hydrogen and oxygen. It concerns us that precious species that have evolved over millions or even billions of years and on which the environment of your planet depends, are being brought close to extinction."

A bell rang and Nantes stood up and left the room.

Maralina: "We are also concerned at the way your atmosphere has been poisoned by over-use of fossils as fuel, when alternative cleaner forms of energy supply have been ignored and, in some cases, suppressed.

"I understand that you also use fossil material for solids in what you call plastic. We use glass, that is made from the substance you call silicon. We can make glass that is stronger than your concrete, and it can also be recycled.

"Most of all we are concerned at your over-dependence on the material chain-reaction that you call nuclear energy.

"Not only is this contaminating in itself, but the proliferation of explosive weapons based on it is one of the main reasons that at present your planet cannot be accepted into the federation of the galaxy.

"It concerns us that some of your political leaders seem concerned with destroying ancient cultures and turning them into piles of rubble, with their citizens being driven from their homes, risking their lives and the lives of their children, causing their families to seek refuge, no longer able to work to improve their lives and that of their people and the environment. We know that you are not directly or personally responsible for this, but we are concerned with the direction of affairs and that this could be spread not only to the Moon but elsewhere."

At this point, Maralina, the Assistant Ambassador, fell silent and nodded almost imperceptibly as though she expected a response.

Maralina: "Please tell us something about yourselves and what it is that you have in mind."

John: "We represent the Halliday Mining Corporation who have covered the cost of these expeditions, in the hope that precious metals and rare minerals can be found."

Maralina: "Oh, so you represent a trading group, not a government, How much does your government know about this?"

John: "Oh yes, they know and have given permission in general terms, but have left sorting the details to our company."

Nantes returned and entered the negotiation room.

Nantes: "Ms assistant ambassador, we have received a message that the Chinese government has just launched a three-person mission that is due to land on the Moon in three days' time."

Maralina: "We had knowledge that such a mission was planned but it was not expected so soon."

Andrew: "It is possible that they have intercepted our messages and may have brought forward their flight, knowing that we are here."

John: "Our Mission Control must know about this Maralina. Is there any way that you can stop them from landing?"

Maralina: "Anything like that could be considered an act of war and that is forbidden under Galaxy Law."

CHAPTER 6

Meanwhile back on Earth, in the JPL Conference Room, there was a meeting underway. Present were Harry and Daniel from the Halliday Corporation and Mark and Owen Miller from NASA.

Harry: "I think we all know why we are here, It is the news that the Chinese government have brought forward their manned Moon mission."

Daniel: "What does NASA think? Could this be because our people are on the Moon at present?"

Mark Wilson: "The question is, do they know that our people are negotiating with the extra-terrestrials? We don't know whether the Chinese have already made contact with the ETs. It seems unlikely, but if they know that we have, they might be up to putting their noses in."

Owen: "We are not going to be able to keep this business under wraps for much longer. It looks like an announcement will have to be made."

Harry: "Do you want us to handle that?"

Mark: "That is what we have to discuss. When dealing with issues at this level the President should really be informed. First, we need to talk this over with NASA Chief, Peter Bridgewater.

"I have been in touch with his secretary and told her about this meeting. She said he will be here in a few minutes."

Peter Bridgewater entered the room.

Mark: "Welcome Mr Bridgewater, I'd like you to meet Harry Wainwright and Daniel Raft, the mission controllers from Halliday mining."

Bridgewater shook hands with them.

Mark: "I invited you here to this meeting because the Chinese government has launched a manned expedition to the Moon and, as you know, we have three astronauts on the Moon at present."

Bridgewater: "Are you suggesting there could be a conflict?"

Owen: "A conflict of interest maybe. What you may not know is that our astronauts have made contact with extra-terrestrials, who have a base on the Moon."

Bridgewater: "No I didn't know that, why wasn't I informed?"

Owen: "That may be our fault. This trip was backed by Halliday as a survey for mining, and it turns out that these extra-terrestrials have been mining on the Moon already."

Bridgewater: "Do you think that the Chinese know this?"

Mark; "We can't rule it out".

Bridgewater: "Then the President should be informed about this."

Mark: "That's what we want to talk to you about. We know that it has been the policy of the Government not to disclose any information about alien contact but under the current circumstances the President might choose to review the situation."

Bridgewater: "Circumstances like this raise security issues. How do we know they are not hostile?"

Harry: "We can't be sure. From the information we have received so far, there are no indications of this but we thought you should know about it. I'll be in touch with the President today and try to arrange a meeting."

Meanwhile, on the Moon, in the oval Negotiation Hall, the ambassador continued with her address.

Maralina: "We are not able to deal with a private trading organisation like yours or with individual governments. We have no wish to create unrest in your world but now your exploration has made contact with our people this needs a level of diplomacy that is unfamiliar to you. The Moon is not quite what you think it is. A long time ago, in ancient times, it was moved here into orbit in order to create the conditions suitable for evolution to happen and life to develop on the planet now called the Earth."

Andrew: "Who moved it here?"

Maralina: "The universe is a lot older than your scientists think and the civilisation who did that have long since departed, but we have traditions and stories telling us how and why it happened."

Julia: "I understand your concerns about weapons, especially nuclear weapons. Have they been used in space before?"

Maralina: "Oh yes but many years ago. Now the technology has developed beyond that. We have the ability to turn off the control systems of your weapons, or if, heaven forbid, the weapons were launched against us, to reverse their path so that they would return and attack the base they had been fired from. However, that is not likely to happen as there is a law throughout the galaxy that forbids it. It is more usual that the weapons would have been disabled in flight and fall harmlessly into the ocean or onto deserted ground. On account of this, channels for negotiation need to be set up and, for this to happen, the governments of the earth need to acknowledge our existence.

"As you now see, the Chinese government is already starting to explore the Moon, and on account of this, our people cannot permit any mining or commercial activities on the Moon until there is agreement and understanding on this issue between the governments of the Earth. You can contact Nantes regarding any further developments. Now, I will be leaving you and saying goodbye."

Maralina stood up and everyone also stood up in a line. She approached each one and they touched hands in silence. Maralina, turned and left the hall.

There were a few moments silence as the Moon people and the astronauts exchanged glances.

Nantes: "She is a great lady. It is a privilege to meet her, she has come a long way to see you".

Rafu: "We have permission to take you on a visit to our workshops. First we offer you some sustenance in liquid form."

Auron wheeled in a trolley with a number of jugs containing liquid of different colours and textures along with ornamental glasses.

Nantes: "Please help yourself and try whichever one you like; they all contain the nutrients necessary for healthy living. When you have finished here, Irgon will go with you to show you round the workshops."

John: "Does that mean that the mining project is off for now?"

Irgon: "Yes I am afraid it does, we cannot do anything more in that respect without the permission of the Embassy. It is this way to the workshops."

They followed Irgon along a passage and down an escalator. Along a second passage was a large window. They could see people working in what looks like a laboratory. Five people were working there, two of them were androids, who looked similar to Auron.

Irgon: "This is where work is done on medical repair and life extension for both human types and for androids. Behind the door at the far end is where the medical equipment is kept and used."

They moved further along to another window.

Irgon: "This is where the gravity equipment is maintained. The craft over there is being serviced."

They could see a circular craft with a section removed.

Andrew: "How do these vehicles work?"

Irgon: "Gravity is an aspect of the natural energy that exists in the universe. By oscillating the frequency, it is possible to create a gravitational field, a flow of gravity if you like.

"Now we will return to the oval hall and you can exchange the clothing for your suits and Auron will return you to the hatch and to the Rover, so you can return to the your LEM."

The astronauts returned to the changing room and donned their space suits again. Auron took them to the cylindrical vehicle they had arrived in and they were transported back to the circular hatch. Outside they returned to the Moon Rover and returned to the LEM and settled down to get some sleep.

The following morning, in Bridgwater's office, Bridgewater was on the phone to the President's Secretary.

Bridgewater: "Hello Ma'am. this is Peter Bridgewater, Head of NASA. Please ask the President if I can have an on-screen chat with him as I have some developments to report."

Secretary: "Yes of course, he's here now, I will set it up for you."

President: "Dominic Carson, United States President here, how can I help?"

Bridgewater: "Mr President, recently we spoke briefly about the mining expeditions to the Moon by the Halliday Corporation. Well things have moved on from that point. On the first trip, the astronauts encountered some extra-terrestrials who are resident on a base inside the Moon and they are already mining there."

President: "Whoa! Oh well that complicates things a bit!"

Bridgewater: "The return trip they made was initially to negotiate a mining arrangement. This was to be with their so-called ambassador who had travelled specially to the Moon for the conference meeting.

"But then came the news that the Chinese government is bringing forward their projected manned landing. This may be the reason that at the conference the Alien Ambassador announced that she could not negotiate with a private trading group or through an individual country, but only with a representative coalition of countries, and she gave as an example the United Nations."

President: "So they know a bit about us then!"

Bridgewater: "She said they have access to our broadcast media and our internet."

President: "Are our astronauts still on the Moon?"

Bridgewater:" No, they are on the way back now."

President: "That is all useful information, is there any other point you wish to raise?"

Bridgewater: "Just whether under the

circumstances, maybe the time has come to announce that extra-terrestrials inhabit the Moon."

President: "I don't think we should rush into that. If our astronauts have left the Moon, there is no possibility of them interacting with the Chinese and I will have to discuss this issue with the CIA and the security people. Thank you again for the information, and keep me informed of any further developments."

After the astronauts returned to Earth, they underwent a brief period of isolation for medical checks and were called up for a debriefing session.

In the JPL conference room, a debriefing session was arranged with John, Andrew and Julia, conducted by Harry and Daniel from Halliday and with Mark and Owen from the JPL.

Mark: "We have your reports from the mission. What is your impression from what happened?"

Julia: "I thought Maralina was a very considerate lady and I can see her point."

Andrew: "It was interesting to see the workshops if only briefly."

John: "Well we were expecting to be there doing a mining survey and it seems that, since the

Chinese arrived, mining is off for now. At the moment we don't seem to be able to move further ahead. We weren't expecting that to happen! We were expecting there to be a mining survey and it seems that mining is now off."

Andrew: "At the moment we don't seem to be much further ahead."

Owen: "Bridgewater has spoken to President Carson and he is going to discuss the reports with the security people.

"There are other things happening too. Since the Chinese landed their three-person team on the Moon, they have been investigating a structure. It includes a mile-high tower that seems to be made of glass."

Andrew: "How do you know this?"

Owen: "We have intercepted their radio signals."

Daniel: "Do you think the Chinese will announce this?"

Mark: "Quite likely they won't. They have been surveying the Moon from satellites for a while and they haven't announced anything about their observations so far."

CHAPTER 7

Meanwhile at the CIA headquarters in Norfolk Virginia, a meeting was in progress between Graham Birkett, CIA Chief, and Paul Ashworth, head of the NSA. They were interviewing Andrew Stevenson, the pilot of the Halliday Moon rocket, and the Moon Rover.

Graham: "Hello Andrew, thank you for coming in. This is Paul Ashworth of the National Security Agency, We have called you in to speak to us today, because the President spoke to me yesterday and explained that during your Moon missions, you encountered a group of extra-terrestrials, aliens to be blunt. He has asked me to investigate the security aspects of this issue, so I have invited Paul along today as well.

"I know that you have been in the Air Force and worked as a test pilot, and that as a result you have security clearance at a high level. We would like to hear your version of what happened both on the Moon and inside the Moon. Are you prepared for giving us that information?"

Andrew: "I will do what I can to help."

Graham: "Fine, go ahead."

Andrew: "Well sir, as I am sure you know, we were on an operation for the Halliday Corporation to assess the possibility of mining on the Moon and in the course of the survey, we found this disk that turned out to be an entrance hatch that we were able to open. In going down the ensuing tunnel, we encountered this android alien who took us to a hall that he referred to as a conference hall. There we were introduced to three more members of staff, who it appears, organise the mining."

Graham: "For us this has quite serious consequences. For many years it has been the policy to deny the existence of extra-terrestrials and this is becoming increasingly more difficult. You see it is our job to protect the security of our country and in this case the whole planet. Regardless of what these beings said to you, we do not know what their agenda is or what their intentions are. So we have no choice but to regard them as possibly hostile.

"I see in the report they have taken exception to our possible use of nuclear power on the Moon and they have a strong disliking of nuclear weapons.

"If we were to surrender our nuclear capability, this would leave us totally vulnerable to attack. It is our duty to submit a report to the President and to propose a policy in this area. As the only astronaut on this project who has been in the military, and so has military experience, I am sure you understand this and we hope you will collaborate with us."

Andrew: "Yes sir."

Graham: "We need to make a survey of any technology they have and their form of communication."

Paul: "The arrival of the Chinese does complicate matters. Suddenly, from being a two-way interaction, it is a six-way interaction. That is, first between us and the ETs, second between the ETs and us, third between us and the Chinese, fourth between the Chinese and us, fifth between the Chinese and the ETs, and sixth between the ETs and the Chinese. The last two are tricky because we are not involved. So you can see that the situation is complicated."

Andrew: "I can see that."

Paul: "The second factor is the Moon's ownership. As you know the Apollo Eleven astronauts planted a Stars and Stripes flag on the Moon. At the time it was stated that this did not mean that the USA was claiming ownership of the Moon but now that could be reconsidered.

"During the cold war, when evidence of alien existence started to become apparent, there was an underlying agreement between Russia and America to shelve their differences in order to face any possible off-world enemy.

"However, there is no evidence that any such similar agreement could be made with the Chinese now, or even if such an agreement was made, whether the Chinese would stick to it."

Graham: "You have met these so-called sky people, do you think that is possible to make a deal with them?"

Andrew: "They were very welcoming and affable but they seem to have some airy-fairy ideas which were different to our scientific thinking, and it was not always possible to work out what they were getting at."

Paul: "We are interested in their science, which in some respects is in advance of ours and for that reason we are not seeking to have a direct confrontation with them, which, apart from anything else, we might lose. But it is now many years since Earth people first landed on the Moon and for this reason, we do consider that the Moon a satellite of the earth and it should really be considered to be part of the domain of the Earth. We do not know who these alien people are where they come from or what their plan is. So this is where you come in. If and when you go back to the Moon, we would like you to ask them some questions. We will supply equipment to record their answers which we can then do a depth analysis on in the hope that if they are truthful, we can get some fix on who or what we are dealing with."

Andrew: "What kind of questions did you have in mind?"

Paul: "We have yet to work that out. There are other parties we will have to consult with, including the military, before we go back to the President with a suggestion for policy."

Andrew: "With all due respect sir, it's John Arland who is the leader of the expedition and he is the negotiator. Also, the last person that we encountered was introduced to us as an ambassador. She is a woman and in negotiating with her it might also be an advantage to have Julia with us. Julia is sensitive to moods and implications and it would I think be useful to have both John and Julia present."

Graham: "We will take account of your views on this matter. We will contact you for the next stage when we are ready."

Andrew stood up and, after saying goodbye to Graham and Paul, left to return to his accommodation.

Graham: "Well Paul what is the view of the NSA on this?"

Paul: "The NSA was originally set up after the Roswell incident. It was our role to prevent people from making illicit contacts with off world beings. That was decades ago. This situation is rather different, It seems that the off-worlders now have possession of the Moon, our Moon. It would be difficult to deny their existence now, already there are rumours flying all around the internet regarding these expeditions."

Graham: "Well we can't deny their existence this time, there has to be some negotiations."

Paul: "The way I see it, this is our Moon. While we did not have access to the Moon, it did not really affect our lives on Earth, but now we do have, we have a right to claim it, and like the Greeks claiming the Elgin Marbles, we want it back. It seems that there is only a handful of beings in residence, however now that we are exploring the Solar System - but we don't want to get nasty.

"We know that we are the only people who have evolved to civilisation level within the Solar System, so we have a right to it. To put it bluntly, we want our Moon back, but we only have the equivalent of bows and arrows and we really don't know what they have."

Graham: "In this report by the astronauts, they quote the aliens as talking about cosmic laws. Maybe we do have rights under cosmic law. If we know what they are, we could use that to our advantage!"

Paul; "Oh yes, for that we would need a lawyer who is conversant with cosmic law, but what is that going to cost us in legal fees?"

Graham: "This woman that the astronauts spoke to was described as a deputy ambassador, so that implies there is some kind of what I can only describe as an interplanetary legal structure. We don't know where they come from, how long they have been there. We need some background on how they regard us."

Paul: "I suggest that we supply the astronauts with a list of questions that we would like replies to and that we record the conversations with them and after that we will have a better idea of who we are dealing with and whether they will give tolerance to our proposals. Another thing they said was that now the Chinese are involved, they will only negotiate with representation from the whole planet and they suggested this could be done through an organisation like the United Nations. Maybe we should talk to the Chinese tell them what is going on and see if we can get them on side."

Graham: "We will have to let the President know what we are doing."

Paul: "Yes of course so the first thing is to lay out a statement for the President."

CHAPTER 8

The following morning, Graham Birkett CIA Chief, and Paul Ashworth, head of the NSA arrived at the White House for a meeting with the President in the Oval Office. They announced themselves to the President's secretary and were issued in.

President Carson: "Morning Gentlemen. The matter you have come to discuss could not be at a higher or more significant level and it has to be handled very delicately. It is nothing less than a negotiation between the leading nations of the world and what I can only call an off-world nation who already occupy our Moon."

Paul: "Yes we understand that Sir, but it seems that the Chinese and possibly even the Russians and also the United Nations would have to be involved. What we propose is that we contact the Chinese Ambassador initially, with your permission, and see if we can make an arrangement that involves the UN. Then, maybe If the Chinese agree to represent Russian interests also, our astronauts could talk to the Space people and see what they have in mind."

President Carson: "That sounds feasible but we still have not found a way of announcing this to the public."

Graham: "No sir, but we think that would be your task to decide when the time is right."

President Carson: "At this point another flight to the Moon would attract attention. Or could anything be done via a video-link?"

Paul. "Yes sir' it could, but first we need to talk to the Chinese. We will get in touch with them and, and talk to the Ambassador tomorrow morning."

President Carson: "That is fine, let me know what happens."

The following morning a meeting had been arranged with the Chinese Ambassador in a conference room in a hotel in Washington. Graham Birkett, CIA Chief, and Paul Ashworth NSA chief were there, along with the Chinese Ambassador, who has brought two aides.

Graham: "Good morning Ambassador Zhau, very pleased to meet you. This is Paul Ashworth of the NSA. We have chosen a neutral space for our meeting because of the very special nature of our subject. No doubt you are aware that our country the United States has recently had two expeditions to the Moon and we are aware that your country has also recently had an expedition to the Moon. First we would like to say that we don't see any conflict in this parallel exploration and to some extent we are prepared to share knowledge. But first we would like to ask you something about your plans and the background of your exploration."

Zhau: "Hello Mr Birkett and Mr Ashworth. Our interest initially, was to take our technology into space. We have been following your work on the Moon and it is of interest to us that you have reported that the gravity is different on different parts of the Moon and that back on November 20, 1969, Apollo 12 deliberately crashed the Ascent Stage of its Lunar Module onto the Moon's surface. NASA reported that the Moon rang like a bell for almost an hour, leading to suggestions that it may be hollow."

Graham: "That leads on to something that we would like to discuss. On our first expedition, the purpose was to look at the possibility of mining the Moon. In the process our astronauts encountered off-world beings already living there and who are apparently mining already."

Zhau: "So, this is the matter you wish to discuss. We had our suspicions, but no proof."

Graham: "It goes further than that. Because of your presence on the Moon, the Aliens' representative has indicated that in order to negotiate with them it is essential for us to collaborate with you and they have suggested working through the United Nations."

Zhau: "I suggest that we work together and discuss how this could best be done before getting the UN involved."

Paul: "Yes I agree with that, there was collaboration between the USA and Russia over the space station. We could look at that and maybe use that as a model."

Graham: "There is a four-way interaction here. We need to consider the relation between our nations, the relation between us and the space people, and the relation with the general public."

Paul: "I don't think many of the general public will be at all surprised if we announce that aliens exist, especially in America. The government has already admitted that in a limited number of incidents, unidentified aerial phenomena or UAP have been reported and they exhibit unusual flight characteristics."

Zhau: "In our country we have observed that as well. If your expeditions have made contact with the space people, we would like more information about this, and if there is another expedition, we would like our astronauts to be there and to make contact with them also."

Paul: "We will put this to the President and suggest that if this proposal is accepted, then this could be the time to announce that there has been contact with the beings from another world."

Two days later, a briefing was issued from the White House that the President was to make a statement in connection with the expeditions to the Moon.

A number of reporters arrived at the White House press briefing room, and among them was Jane Westgate.

There were other people there as well who Jane assumed were from the security services and some people who were most likely from Halliday Mining, which had funded the expeditions. There was a lectern on the dais with two microphones attached. A member of the White House press staff walked up to it and announced that the President was about to speak.

President Carson: "Fellow Americans, what I have to say today will come as a surprise to some of you. It came as a surprise to me. To come directly to the point, the astronauts who recently travelled to the Moon on a mining expedition encountered an alien presence when they were there. Two of the astronauts were taken into a room that is under the Moon's surface. Three beings that they met were of human appearance. There was one who was slightly shorter and who they could only describe as having an appearance similar to what is referred to as a Grey. This has obvious implications for Halliday's mining project and further implications for the Earth as a whole. It was decided to inform the Chinese government of this circumstance as they also have their own astronauts who recently have landed on the Moon. We have no further information at present as to who they are or where they come from. Since they come from outside the solar system, their technology is obviously more advanced than ours. Our astronauts described their meeting as pleasant and sociable and in no way threatening. Any questions?"

Jane raised her hand.

Jane: "How does this effect the plan for mining the rare earth metals in the Moon?"

President Carson: "We hope that that will continue but for the time being it has been delayed."

Richard, another reporter put up his hand.

President Carson: "Yes?"

Richard: "Does this mean that the military could become involved?"

President Carson: "The military and the security services have been informed of the situation but at present we do not anticipate military action or anything of that nature. However, first we have more work to do in talking to the Chinese about the whole issue.

"As there are no more questions, we are ending the press conference. When we have more information, we will issue a press statement."

Jane returned to the National Investigator office to discuss the issue with her editor.

Jane: "Morning Edward, the President has just announced that the astronauts on the Moon mission have encountered aliens on the Moon!"

Edward: "That is brilliant news! We have an edition coming out tomorrow. If you write up the story now, we'll put it on the front page."

Jane: "Oh, I will do that. And I have been looking into the way that astronauts are recruited. They are looking for people who can pass the medical tests, and who have the qualifications they are looking for, like geologists and astronomers. There is also a vacancy for a journalist, and I am thinking of applying.

Edward: 'That sounds good, and if you get in you could write a story for us about your training.'

The next morning, National appeared on the news-stands heading with the story.

THE PRESIDENT ANNOUNCES THAT THE ASTRONAUTS HAVE MET ALIENS ON THE MOON

'From the White House briefing room, the President has announced that two of the astronauts, John Arland and Andrew Stevenson who travelled to the Moon, had an encounter with *four beings from space. Three were of human appearance and one who was described as an android type. The astronauts were led to a room that was beneath the surface of the Moon. Later they were released and returned to Earth. As a result of this meeting, the plans for mining minerals on the Moon have been put on hold. The American military and Intelligence authorities have been notified. At present, no military action or anything of that nature is anticipated. The Chinese have recently had their astronauts land on the Moon, and currently there are negotiations on this issue going on between the American and Chinese authorities'.*

Soon all the media and radio stations were buzzing with the news. The switchboards at Halliday and NASA were hot with enquiries from journalists and the public.

Graham Birkett, CIA Chief, and Paul Ashworth NSA chief met in conference and resumed their negotiations with Chinese ambassador Zhau.

Graham: "We raised the issue of mining on the Moon with the space people but their representative said that they could not negotiate with a company or even with a country. Negotiation had to be with a group that represents the whole of the planet earth and they have suggested this could be through the UN."

Ambassador Zhau: "This could be possible but we would need more information about what is happening and what has been discussed. Would it be feasible for our representatives to meet your astronauts?"

Graham: "I would have to discuss that with the President. Although the mission was funded by Halliday mining, NASA is now involved. On account of the current situation, the next step would be contact between NASA and the body that represents China's interests, which I understand is the China National Space Administration, the CNSA."

Ambassador Zhau: "There are three agencies in China that deal with matters of space. There is China National Space Administration or CNSA, The China aerospace and Technology Corporation, and China Manned Space Agency, the CMSA, who operate the manned space program. These all work together but in this situation, it might be better if it is initially handled by the CMSA. Then there is also the Russian Space Agency, Roscosmos, who NASA already have dealings with in connection with the International Space Station."

Paul: "I see what you are getting at now, you are suggesting that we need an international group, a bit like the UN who can deal with matters of space,"

Ambassador Zhau: "Yes, it would be similar to an embassy that represents the whole of the planet Earth, toward the space people that your astronauts have met. But then there may even be other cultures from other planets and other solar systems. The first thing that the Chinese government would like to ask your space people is whether there are other space cultures out there. We would not like to get involved in an interplanetary war just because we have teamed up with the wrong side. It seems that since they are making demands on us, it is fair that we can make requests of them."

Paul: "So far the only people who have spoken to them are our astronauts. Mainly the lead astronaut John Arland who, since returning, has spoken to them by video link. We would prefer it if he was the one who put your questions to them. I will try and arrange a meeting, so that you can then give him your questions."

The following morning, Graham and Paul arrived with John Arland and Andrew Stevenson. Ambassador Zhau arrived with Chen, who represented the China Manned Space Agency. Graham introduced them to each other.

Chen: "Could you tell us something about your meeting?

John: "When we landed on the Moon, we started doing a survey and we came across a trapdoor on the ground. We opened it and found a tunnel that we started to explore. When we returned to it, it was closed and locked.

"So we went down the tunnel again looking for another way out. We eventually found another door that was opened by an android, who said his name was Auron. He took us on a sleigh-like vehicle down a further tunnel and then we were taken through an airlock to a room where he said it was safe to remove our helmets. There we met three human types. They talked about their philosophy and explained that they already had a mining project on the Moon.

Chen: "Did they tell you who they were or where they came from?"

John: "No they didn't, They just gave us their names, and mentioned what their role was on the Moon."

Ambassador Zhau: "Yet they said that they could not deal with an individual company or with or with just one country, but only with an organisation that represented the whole of planet earth."

Andrew: "That was later, on our second mission, when we met a lady who was described as a deputy ambassador, after we had raised the question as to whether there was any prospect of us being able to do any mining there. That was after the news broke that your Chinese Moon mission had landed."

Graham: "We could then see that to get any further, we would have to make contact with you and your government."

Paul: "If we could present a united front to the space people, to show that we had some coordination between us, we might make some further progress.

"As you mentioned previously, we would not want to team-up with the wrong side, they probably feel the same way."

Ambassador Zhau: "It is much too early to try and involve everybody. Maybe a select group, more like the security council; but even to do that, we need to have more information about who we are dealing with. It has been mentioned that you would prefer it if astronaut John dealt with the space people initially, so I am asking you John, if you could gather some more information about who they are, where they come from, who else is out there, and what their plan is."

John: "If that is what the president, NASA and the security people want to know, then I will do what I can. I will work with Paul and Peter Bridgewater, the Chief NASA administrator, but I need to get security clearance for that to happen as soon as possible."

A few days later, the three astronauts were back at the NASA headquarters in the communications room with a view to making contact with the space people. Present were John Arland, Peter Bridgewater, NASA chief, and a technician. It was decided that initially John would make the contact alone.

Technician: "Shall I use the same connection line that was used before?"

John: "Yes please"

They watched as the screen lights up. It stayed blank.

After a few moments John spoke.

John: "This is John the Astronaut here. I wish to speak to Auron."

There was some flashing and crackling from the screen and after a minute or so, they heard Auron's voice.

Auron: "Hello John, this is Auron speaking, tell me how I can help?"

John: "At our last contact with your Deputy Ambassador, she said that your people would only deal with an organisation that represented the whole of the planet Earth. So as a result, we have contacted the Chinese Ambassador, who also claims to represent the Russian interest. As a result of this meeting, it was decided to come back to you and ask for more information about things such as who you are, where you come from and about your agenda."

Auron: "For that you need to talk to Nantes.

"His concern is the diplomacy and negotiation with other beings who are living in the universe and with those in our galaxy. He is here and he is ready to speak with you."

John: "Hello Nantes, are you there?"

Nantes: "Hello John, Yes. I can give you some of the information that you are requesting. For many years our people have had what your people call mother ships. These are self-contained in space. For example, our craft can approach a star and be regenerated from the light and heat given out from it. There are many communities in the galaxy, We have now been active on the Moon for more than two hundred of your earth years. Our home planet is in the constellation that you call the Pleiades. It is in a stellar system similar to the Earth's. Although the Pleiades are over 40 light years away, it is considered to be in the same region of your solar system.

"Since you arrived on the Moon, we have been expecting your people to ask questions like these, and we have information on how such matters as these are dealt with on your planet Earth.

"There have been many interactions between space people and Earth people in the past. The ancient pre-technology cultures on the earth understood how to live with and work with nature better than is happening now.

"We see that legal and accounting approaches are affecting the environment planet in a damaging way. Space people cannot expect to change this, it is up to the earth people to sort this out.

"There is concern among some communities of space people that if you were to discover our technology you might take your nuclear weapons out into space to use them on us. Although we have the technology to prevent this happening, this is not the way that things are done in the local galaxy community. We also know that some of your space exploration has been done for a military purpose.

"Your governments have had plenty of opportunity to recognise the existence of the space people but they continually refused to do so. Is this because they assume that we are aggressive and hostile? Had we had the intention to harm the human race we have had the ability to do so for many aeons. The reverse is the case. Our interest is to extend our knowledge and understanding, not to create military empires. For us, these are negative thoughts and can only lead to disaster.

"We are also aware that your people might think that we are only saying these things to lull you into a false sense of security so that we can take advantage of you in a weak moment, but nothing could be further from the truth. We have immortal consciousness. For us the universe is infinite, eternal and self-regenerating."

John: "How can that be so?"

Nantes: "I can tell that you are confused by the idea but I can demonstrate to you that you are also an immortal spiritual being. Relax, rest back and watch me."

Through the screen Nantes stared into John's eyes.

Nantes: "Now gently, be above your body."

John could feel the experience of rising above his body. He could look down at the top of his body's head. He could look round the room and in that moment a veil lifted for John and he came to realise that he had become a spirit that was separate from his body.

John: "Yes, I am back in my body now and I understand what you mean but I need to walk about a bit to get adjusted to that experience and go and get a drink of water."

After a short period, John returned.

Nantes: "Do you now have a better understanding of the idea?"

John: "It was like a new experience for me, I feel that I am no longer just an interviewer, but a trusted friend. I feel safer now, it is like I have come home."

Nantes: "I also feel similar things. This is part of our culture and our science and the culture of other communities that you may call the space people. There is now hope for greater understanding between us.

"We would like to see the Moon as a place where such things can be shared.

"This is a stepping point for you and also for us. This is our science. For us there is no empty space, as the universal life energy is everywhere.

John: "That was a remarkable thing that I just did and the fact that you can take me into that experience from over two hundred thousand miles away."

Nantes: "You did it yourself, I put the suggestion in your mind in a way that distance is not a factor."

John: "Yes I understand that. But the people who approached me to talk to you asked for more information than that. They asked me to gather information about who you are, where you come from, who else is out there and what your plans are."

Nantes: "Some of this I have already explained. But I can cover it more deeply, and in greater detail. Many people have travelled far across the galaxy and so come from different constellations. Rafu for example comes from a different constellation that is far away, though still in this same galaxy. There are different regions in the galaxy and the one we are from is based in the constellation of the Pleiades.

"These regions or states communicate with each other and trade with each other. Language is not a problem as telepathy is common. It is our task to introduce you to, and eventually to bring you into, this region. For this to happen, the first stage is for your people to learn that we exist. This has already begun with your President's announcement but this is just the beginning. There is distrust and hostility among your people. It was thought from our side that the crop circles would help open a way to understanding, and this did happen for a while.

"When the time and conditions are right, the Deputy Ambassador of our region is prepared to come down to Earth and meet and liaise with your leaders, to further the peaceful interaction of our peoples. I now feel that our meeting is coming to an end, do you have any further questions?"

John:" Thank you for this information. My superiors will have a recording of our interaction. I have nothing further to ask at the moment, so I will just say goodbye".

Nantes: "As your friends in France and in Quebec say, au revoir."

CHAPTER 9

Two days later in the same hotel conference room, Graham of the CIA, Paul of the NSA, Ambassador Zhau, astronauts John and Andrew, Philip from NASA and Peter Bridgewater, head of NASA had gathered.

Peter: "You have all heard the recording of John's interview with Nantes, from the Moon. Who would like to go First?"

Paul: "After the President's announcement, there isn't any going back. We will have to bite the bullet."

Graham: "Hardly an appropriate metaphor! Anyhow, I am interested in the piece about the alien deputy ambassador visiting Earth. There's a lot of work to do before that could happen. What does Ambassador Zhau think?"

Ambassador Zhau: "Yes a lot of work but let us look at the possible outcome. It could be an event that would bring us together, make a lot of publicity, and change our relationship with the Space People. We would prefer it to happen on neutral territory."

Peter Bridgewater; "What about Diego Garcia? It is

a British protectorate but on loan to the United States Military. But it is in Indian Ocean and almost equidistant from Africa, India, Arabia and Australia."

Ambassador Zhau: "That is possible but we would prefer somewhere in the Pacific Ocean."

Graham: "We can suggest the venue later, a military base would be an advantage form the security point of view."

Paul: "We need more information about what this means in terms of recognition between the Earth and the Space People, we don't even have a name for them yet."

John: "We don't know whether they will allow us to mine there."

Peter Bridgewater: "I think that NASA would handle part of that and I also think it is time to involve the United Nations, which was originally set up with a view to becoming a world government."

Paul: "Does this mean that there will be a Space Ambassador somewhere on the Earth?"

Peter Bridgewater: "That is more likely to be on the Moon. Once it has been set up, maybe there will be an opportunity for exchange of information. Although it seems they know a lot about us, we don't know much about them. If Diego Garcia is used it should be demilitarised. It would not be appropriate to have it bristling with military equipment! How about somewhere near Australia, like Tasmania, or how about New Zealand?"

Graham: "What are airports and airbases like in New Zealand?"

Paul looking at a screen, "Ohakea air base looks like the most suitable. At present it is used for training and for helicopters. It's on the North Island and is used by marine patrol aircraft. It has civil aircraft facilities and can be used as a support point for Wellington airport if needed. On the north island, it's a hundred miles north of the capital Wellington, which is on the southern point of the north island."

Ambassador Zhau: "New Zealand is a place that would be acceptable to us."

Peter Bridgewater: "We will need to talk to the New Zealand government to see if we can get permission to use it. Then to the United Nations and to the European Union. I can approach them initially as NASA will be involved. I suggest that we close this meeting now and reconvene this time next week and then I will report on how things have gone."

A week later in the same hotel room.

Peter Bridgewater: "Good morning everyone, we have three new members today. Let me bring in the New Zealand ambassador, a representative from the United Nations, and an emissary from the European Union.

"Together with John, I have now also contacted Nantes on the link to the Space People. He said that their representative would address us all on the video link. I am sure many of you will have questions to ask.

"I suggest we retire to the rest room and return when the engineers have finished setting up the equipment."

Half an hour later, the delegates filed into the conference room, and took their places.

A picture opened up on the screen showing the Moon as background, the four persons, Irgon, Rafu, Nantes and Auron, were standing in a semi-circle.

Nantes: "We are very happy to be invited to speak to your committee and to give you our Deputy ambassador. I would like to introduce you all to Maralina, who is the deputy ambassador of our home planetary system."

The group of four separated and Maralina walked in between them and looked around.

Maralina: "We are hoping that our meeting can eventually lead to a constructive outcome between our civilisations. We acknowledge that you have a claim to the Moon due to its being a satellite of the Earth and that your people should eventually be permitted access and use of it.

"We especially welcome the representative of the Nation of China, a very ancient culture, who have now shown that they also have the capability to reach the Moon. Also the representatives of the European Union and of the United Nations. We have many aspects of our culture to offer to you, as you do to our culture. We especially like your music! We appreciate your invitation to visit you in New   Zealand.

"But for now, the time is not yet ready. Maybe in two or three years when both your culture and ours have adjusted to the new situation and things have settled down, we might be able to do so. Meanwhile we are happy to accept peaceful exploration of the Moon's surface. Now I will leave you and Nantes can answer all your questions."

Maralina turned to the group, bowed and left.

Nantes stepped forward.

Nantes: "Maralina is a great person, respected across the galaxy."
John: Is the mining still going on?"

Nantes: "Not now, the mining has been stopped."

Julia Brownlow: "What is the status of women in your society?"

Nantes: Women and men are the same. There is no difference except that women have special status regarding childbirth and caring for the family."

Ambassador Zhau: "Do you have different races, different skin colour, different heights, or other physical differences?"

Nantes: "There are differences but these are appreciated as cultural differences."

Graham: "How do you regard us?"

Nantes: "I would like to give you an example, When your people were exploring the rainforests on different continents, you would sometimes encounter tribes that had not made contact with western people. Sometimes they were hostile and aggressive.

"There are similarities between your relationship with them and our relationship with you but we hope that these meetings will give rise to a greater understanding."

Peter: "What about the technology you have?"

Nantes: "Our approach to science is different to yours. We have known for a long time about the chain reaction between large atoms that can give rise to nuclear explosions and these still exist in your society, whereas these have not been used and been outlawed for a long time in our culture. Until this law is accepted by your people, we cannot fully share that aspect of our culture with you."

New Zealand ambassador: "It was considered that your representative would come to Earth and New Zealand was proposed as a landing and meeting place."

Nantes: "This has been discussed with the group including Maralina and, although New Zealand is well thought of and a meeting there could be successful, it was thought that, as things are, it is not yet safe enough for us to make a visit to Earth.

"In place of that, we would welcome a collective visit to the Moon. If different countries would be happy to send their astronauts and their representatives to the Moon, we could all have a meeting here. The Moon could become a place where astronauts from different countries could collaborate in the same way that there was collaboration between astronauts of different countries on the international space station.

"Now if there are no more questions, I will say thank you for our meeting and until the next time, we will sign off."

The screen went blank.

Graham: "Well, what do people think about that lot?"

Paul: "Well it sounds like they are not very keen on visiting earth."

Julia: "That does not surprise me, considering the complexities down here."

Paul: "It seems like they are offering to open up the Moon on certain conditions. We don't have a lot of choice, if we wish to continue to explore the Moon, but to agree and comply with their conditions."

Ambassador Zhau: "If our astronauts are going to on the Moon for more than a few days, we will need facilities there, we will need to talk to them about what is available."

Paul: "If we could get a reporter into the astronaut crew that would be a big help."

Peter: "There is a reporter who was accepted by NASA for astronaut training and who is doing well. Her name is Jane Westgate. It might be possible to accelerate her training but we do not know yet what the time scale is, for all of this project to happen."

Bridgewater: "We are going to have to work out a plan to deal with all this, and then present it to the President. Maybe we could send a representative team to stay on the Moon for a few weeks as guests of the space people to sort out agreements for larger and more permanent arrangement."

Graham: "If we could send up a vehicle that could be used a living accommodation and as an HQ, we would have our own facilities for experiments and exploration.

"This could also be used as a setting off point for any manned expeditions to Mars or elsewhere. It could be very useful to have a telescope on the Moon that is manned and that is clear of the Earths' atmosphere."

Paul: "How about a glass dome that could be used for growing plants for food? Then it would start to look like a more permanent settlement and this might give the project more appeal to the President."

Ambassador Zhau: "This idea of a glass dome appeals to us though we did not have the opportunity to participate in the International Space Station. We hope to be given the opportunity to collaborate in this project."

Paul: "I suggest that a report is prepared on everything that has been discussed both between us and the Space people and that this report is delivered and presented to the President. I imagine he will go through it with his people and give us a response. Also funding will have to be allocated before going to the next stage."

Over the next four months there were plans for three Moon expeditions, American, European and Chinese. The European expedition would include German and French astronauts. The Chinese expedition would include Russian astronauts.

The journalist Jane Westgate who had completed the astronaut training would be travelling to the moon as part of the American expedition. Although the European space agency hadn't yet made a landing on the moon. They had already established an orbital space station and would be arriving later than the others on their first moon landing expedition.

Meanwhile, the Space people, in conjunction with the Chinese and American space agencies, had decided on a location where the base would be situated. It was to be close to the Moon's equator, on the side that is visible to the Earth, whereas the Space people's main base was on the reverse side that cannot be seen from the Earth.

It would be a further three months before the Chinese and American spacecraft were ready to take off. The three original astronauts had been joined by David White, who had previously been the orbiter pilot, at the base. There was no need for an orbiter as they would not be travelling back to Earth in the short term.

As the American astronauts lined up before ascending on to the spacecraft, Jane Westgate, now qualified as an astronaut and who was the media representative on the crew, joined them and was being interviewed by a presenter from National Television.

Presenter: "Well Jane, after the stories you have given us an account of your training and about the development of the project, how does it feel to be finally Setting off for the moon?"

Jane: "As you can imagine, it's a mixture of excitement and anxiety. After six months of training and preparation, I feel a lot of responsibility as it's the first time that a journalist has been part of a space travel project like this. Although I have spoken to the space people on a telescreen, this will be the first time I will have a chance to meet them in the flesh, if indeed you can say that! Once we have left the Earth's orbit, I may be able to give you a report while we are travelling towards the moon. After that there will be only reports from the pilot to mission control until we have landed safely on the moon. Finally, I would like to say thank you to my co-travellers on this journey, John, Andrew, Julia and David."

The Astronauts nodded to the camera when Jane mentioned their names. They then headed toward the lift to take them to the flight deck of the ship.

Two hours later the countdown began and Andrew, as the pilot prepared for lift-off. Then, with a huge roar, the massive ship took off.

Two hours into the flight, Jane made a broadcast.

Jane: "Hello everybody. Now we are here heading for the moon. Everything is going to plan. As the craft lifted off, the acceleration was so strong you have the experience of being pushed down onto your back. I have experienced it before in training but this is the first time I have experienced it in an actual space craft. We can just see the whole of Earth. We have one more rocket boost to make, as we are still under the effect of the earth gravity, then we will be coasting. We are travelling steadily but in eighteen hours' time the moon will be pulling us towards itself and we will start be travelling faster again, accelerating toward the moon under the influence of the moon's own gravity."

Two days later, the retro-rockets brought them down and, as they descended and they approached the agreed landing area, the crew with Jane were astonished with what they could see. Magnificent geometric patterns spreading out from and around the agreed landing site, were glowing and glittering. In some parts of the pattern were shelters with doors arranged in a semicircle. Andrew gently lowered the craft into the appointed place. The astronauts stepped down from the craft.

From the doors emerged the Space people that the astronauts had already met on previous visits, Irgon, Nantes and Rafu, wearing light coloured space suits.

Nantes: "Welcome you all, we now see you as the deputation representing the all the people of the Earth."

Nantes stepped forward holding out both of his hands and touched both of John's hands and the hands of the other astronauts in a salute of welcome.

Rafu: "The patterns that you saw when you came down to land represent the unity and harmony between all the people of the universe, as it is our goal that the moon should be a place for all the beings from wherever they are, to live and study in peace and harmony together for all time."

Irgon: "We have ceased all mining on the moon, because it is more important for the moon to be used for bringing together the people of the Earth with the Space communities of which we are a part. And now we would like to lead you back into the moon to meet with our Deputy ambassador Maralina who is looking forward to seeing you again and who will present a more detailed vision of how things can evolve."

Nantes guided them to another door and they went down a stairway to where the sleigh-like vehicle guided by Auron, was waiting for them. The crew greeted Auron and they set off along the tunnel.

After about fifteen minutes, the sleigh arrived at a platform and they were directed off and along a passageway and through an airlock to a changing room. They were invited to remove their suits. There were cupboards containing robes and clothes from which they could choose to wear what they wished. The Space people did the same.

Nantes: "Maralina is waiting to greet you in the Hall of Reception along with other dignitaries from the Nation of the Pleiades, our home constellation."

The crew with Jane, accompanied by the Space people, walked along a corridor into the Reception Hall, a large oval space decorated with coloured geometrical patterns. Before them was a reception committee with Maralina in the centre and with a dozen dignitaries on each side.

They walked through the gap between chairs and other seating equipment and were signalled to sit down. Maralina began to speak.

Maralina: "In the thousands of years during which our ancestors have been exploring and travelling throughout the galaxy, we have always been keen to spread the peace and joy that we have experienced in our culture.

"We know that that there has been pain and distress among your earth peoples, and we would like to say that it does not have to be like that and that we would like to dedicate the Moon as a place that is dedicated to the growth and well-being of a culture of understanding, tolerance and knowledge.

"There are many things that you Earth people have yet to learn in that respect, and to practise among your own people. We can help you with that, and when the people of the Earth have learned to respect our laws there is the chance for you to become as we are, fully-accepted citizens of the galaxy.

"The Chinese delegation will soon arrive with their friends the Russians and will settle in the community of the space settlers which will eventually include the Indian nation and the other nations who wish to travel here. The Moon can then become a beacon of peace for all of your world and will signal a tone for that to unify and bless the generations of peace that will follow."

At that point a glorious sound filled the hall and a sense of belief in the unity of all things and of all people and enveloped all the people there.

After Maralina had finished her speech, the crew members and Jane lined up to greet the dignitaries, holding out their hands and touching the dignitaries' hands by way of greeting and recognition.

After the speech and the celebration, the astronauts returned to their space vehicle. They sat down in a circle.

Jane: "How do you feel after that?"

John: "It was amazing to have been present at this moment, that may well turn out to be a great moment in our history."

David: "This was my first time of being on the surface of the moon and I had not met any of the Space people before. Also hearing Maralina speak, this for me, was an experience that was very literally out of this world!!"

The crew then took some rest in after what had been a long day.

The following morning, Jane prepared to make a broadcast to announce their landing.

Jane: "We have had a most remarkable welcome to the moon. As we were coming down to land, we found that the agreed landing area was encircled by a most beautiful giant shimmering pattern. It was like the largest and most magnificent crop circle I'd ever seen and from doors within the pattern emerged the Space people that our astronaut friends had met before on their earlier visits to the moon.

"After the initial greeting, we were taken down to an underground vehicle that took us to a magnificent oval hall of welcome. After we had changed out of our space suits, we were addressed by Maralina who was introduced to us as the deputy ambassador of the Pleiades.

"Maralina explained to us that the philosophy of the galaxy was joy and peace and that the Moon would from now on be a symbol of hope joy and peace for the Earth people and the people from space.

"She also told us that in ancient time, the Moon had been placed into the position where it would encircle the Earth thirteen times every year so it would appear from Earth to be exactly the same size as the Sun. This was to create the perfect conditions for the evolution of a wide range of plants and animals and it was hoped that an intelligent race would evolve and they would take care of the planet and the species that have evolved on it.

"She also said that if the nations of the Earth could agree to make peace with each other they would share their technology with us and that would enable us to solve the environment and other problems that we on the earth have."

Two days later an announcement was made by the President from the Oval Office in the White House.

President Carson: "I have an important announcement to make today that may affect all of our lives. It concerns the Moon and all of the nations of the earth. As you may know, since the original landing of the Halliday project ship many things have happened. The crew were gracefully received by the residents of the Moon, who we will now refer to as the Space People. Since the Chinese people landed on the Moon, the Space People have been in touch with the Chinese people and with the Russians, people of India and Africa, the Europeans and the Arabian nations.

"All have agreed that from now on the Moon will be established as a place for peace and co-operation between the people of Space and the people of the Earth. No weapons of any sort will be permitted on the moon.

"Peace and co-operation is the language and culture of the peoples of deep space. Through the agency of the United Nations, we have now been able to make agreements about this with all the governments of the world that the moon will become a place for international and Inter-global peace and co-operation.

Steven Pank 2024

MORE BOOKS ON AMAZON AND KINDLE FROM ABeFree PUBLISHING

https://www.buffry.org.uk/abefreepublishing.html